Richard Wagner, Anna Alice Chapin

**The Story of the Rhinegold**

(Der Ring des Nibelungen) Told for Young People

Richard Wagner, Anna Alice Chapin

**The Story of the Rhinegold**
*(Der Ring des Nibelungen) Told for Young People*

ISBN/EAN: 9783337019075

Printed in Europe, USA, Canada, Australia, Japan

Cover: Foto ©Andreas Hilbeck / pixelio.de

More available books at **www.hansebooks.com**

WOTAN AND BRÜNNHILDE

THE

# STORY OF THE RHINEGOLD

## (DER RING DES NIBELUNGEN)

### Told for Young People

BY

ANNA ALICE CHAPIN

ILLUSTRATED

NEW YORK AND LONDON
HARPER & BROTHERS PUBLISHERS
1900

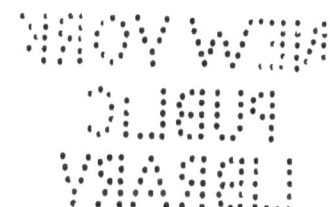

TO

**THE MASTER'S DAUGHTER**

EVA WAGNER

WITH HEARTFELT GRATITUDE

FOR HER KINDNESS AND ENCOURAGEMENT

THIS BOOK

Je Dedicated

# PREFACE

*The Story of the Rhinegold* contains the four operas of Richard Wagner's "Nibelungen Ring," arranged for young people. The "Nibelungen Ring," or "Nibelungen Cycle," is built upon a colossal foundation: a number of the great Teutonic myths, welded together with the most masterly skill and consistency. It is evident that Wagner, like William Morris and other writers, has taken from the fragmentary mythological tales such material as would serve his purpose, adapting such incidents as he chose and as he considered appropriate to his work. But there are so many different versions of these old stories that it is very difficult to trace Wagner's plot to its original birthplace. The various tales contained in the ancient sagas are so seemingly contradictory that anything connectedly authoritative appears impossible to trace. The one thing which seems to remain the same in almost all versions of the stories, ancient and modern, is the background of mythology, that great, gloomy cycle of gods, with the ever-recurring note of Fate which seems to have impressed all searchers in myths alike, and which inspired Wagner when he formed his mystical, solemn Fate motif.

Odin, Wuotan, Wodin, or Wotan, according to the different names given him in the old legends, is the central figure in the framework. If I read the story aright, the Norns, or more properly Nornir, are next in importance. They and their mother, the Vala, are the medium through which the relentless something behind the gods made itself felt in the world. The three sisters are named respectively *Urdr*, *Verdandi*, and *Skuld*—freely translated Past, Present, and Future; or, as they were once styled, as correctly perhaps, Was, Is, and Shall Be. It is a question whether Erda and Urdr, the oldest Norn, might not originally have been identical. Dr. Hueffer speaks of Erda as the "Mother of Gods and Men," but though "the Vala" is often found in mythology, the name Erda is rarely mentioned, whereas the titles for the three Norns seem to be unquestionably correct. The term *Vala* is usually translated as Witch, or Witch-wife, but, though a Vala was indeed a sorceress, she was a prophetess as well.

A step lower than the gods, yet gifted with supernatural power and far removed from the characteristics of human beings, were the dwarfs and the giants. The giants, we are told, were creatures belonging properly to the Age of Stone, which explains the fact that there were left but two representatives of the race at the time of the Golden Age. The dwarfs come under the head of elves. They were gifted with the utmost cleverness and skill. The giants were stupid and clumsy, and, save for their superhuman strength and size, entirely inferior to the small, sly dwarfs.

The world was strangely peopled in those days; many of the heroes were demi-gods, that is, descended from some god or goddess, and witches, dwarfs, and sorcerers mingled with human beings.

Many mortals, also, had magic power then. Otter, the son of Rodmar, changed himself into the animal for which he was named, and while in the shape of the otter he was caught and killed by three of the gods who were wandering over the earth in disguise. Rodmar demanded weregild,* and Loki, with a net, caught Andvari, a rich and malignant dwarf, and commanded him to pay a ransom of gold and gems, enough to cover the skin of the otter; for such was the weregild demanded by Rodmar. Andvari, of necessity, gave the gold for his own release, even adding a wonderful wealth-breeding Ring to cover up a single hair in the skin which the rest of the treasures had left unconcealed. The dwarf cursed the Ring, and the curse attended it through all its manifold ways of magic, to the end of the story.

Rodmar's remaining sons, Fafnir and Regin, killed their father and fought for the treasure. Fafnir obtained it, and, turning himself into a monster-worm, went to Glistenheath (sometimes called Glittering Hearth) to guard his wealth. Regin called upon Sigurd, a young hero, to aid him, and, being a master-smith, forged for him a sharp sword named Gram. Some versions give the forging of the sword to Sigurd, but there are many sides to the story. The sword was sometimes called Gram, and oftener Baldung, until Wagner gave it the more expressive

---

* *Weregild* is almost untranslatable. It may mean payment, tax, forfeit, or ransom.

name of Nothung, or Needful. Prompted by
Regin, Sigurd slew the Dragon at Glistenheath,
and, after tasting the blood by accident, was
able to understand the language of birds, and
was told by two of Odin's ravens that Regin was
treacherous. After slaying Regin, Sigurd rode
away with two bundles of the treasures slung
across his horse's back. He found and awakened Brynhildr, a beautiful woman asleep in a
house on a hill. (She is known in the different
tales in which she has figured as Brynhildr, Brunhild, Brunehault, and Brünnhilde.) The next
part of the tale is most clearly set forth in the
" Nibelungenlied," an epic poem in Middle High
German dialect, containing a story — or, more
correctly, a series of stories — which originally
belonged to the entire Teutonic people. These
have been found in multitudinous poems and
sagas, from those written by the ancient Norse-
men, and most primitive in form, to the modern
books, essays, and poems of writers who have
been impressed with the interesting and picturesque aspects of the strange, complicated old
story. The "Nibelungenlied" itself deals rather
with the period of Christianity—with the knights
and ladies of the time of chivalry—than with the
primeval gods and heroes of the Golden Age.

The substance of its contents may be found in the "Edda" and in the "Thidrekssaga " (thirteenth century), and the original manuscripts of the "Nibelungenlied" itself date from the thirteenth to the sixteenth century.

The story contained in this poem is, briefly told, as follows:

Siegfried, son of Siegmund and Sieglind, woos Kreimhild, the sister of King Gunther, of Burgundy, promising, in return for her hand, to aid Gunther in winning Brunhild, Queen of Issland (Iceland). Siegfried, with the help of his cloud-cloak, conquers Brunhild for Gunther—first in three athletic games, which she makes a test for all suitors; and later when, after the marriage, she proves stormy and untamed. He takes her Ring and girdle, and gives them to his wife, Kreimhild. They possess magic properties, and Brunhild, when deprived of them, loses her great power and becomes like any ordinary woman. She sees her Ring on Kreimhild's hand one day, and, realizing that it is Siegfried, and not her husband Gunther, who has conquered her great strength and stolen her magic circlets, she tells her wrongs to Hagan, who promises revenge. Hagan is the Knight of Trony, and he and his brother Dankwort are Gunther's vassals.

Hagan entices Kreimhild to reveal to him the secret of her husband's safety in battle, and she tells him that Siegfried once slew a dragon and bathed in the blood, which made him invulnerable, save in one place, between his shoulders, where a leaf fell, protecting the skin from the blood. Kreimhild is entirely deceived by Hagan, and, not suspecting his treachery, she sews a circle of silk upon her husband's vesture over the vulnerable spot, that Hagan may better know how to protect the hero's one weakness when they are in battle. It is there, where the circle of silk is sewn, that Hagan stabs him.

There is much more in the "Nibelungenlied," and a character famous in poesy and sagas is introduced later in the poem—Atli, or Attila, King of the Huns; but he has nothing to do with our story, though some one has drawn a resemblance between his character and that of Hunding. The "Nibelungenlied," after Siegfried's death, contains very little connected in any way with Wagner's four operas.

There are other versions of this tale, as there are of all ancient stories. There are many tales of the killing of the Dragon and the awakening of Brunhild, and the personality and history of the latter have passed under diverse alterations in color and development. One story says that Brynhildr, the Valkyrié, was made to slumber by her father Odin, who pricked her in the temple with a sleep-thorn. Many writers tell of a fire-circle which surrounded the sleeper and guarded her slumbers. She is known as a great queen, a woman gifted with magic powers, and a disobedient Walküre in different tales; and her character changes as constantly as her history in the various legends where we read of her. Sigurd, Siegfried, and Sinfiotli are, in many respects, so similar that they might safely be termed identical, though sometimes, as in William Morris's "Sigurd, the Volsung," they appear as distinct characters.

Out of this confused and complicated sea of myths, legends, and old Norse stories Wagner has drawn the material for his wonderful cycle.

His gods and goddesses are taken, with very few changes, directly from their original place—the Teutonic mythology. His giants and dwarfs are also unaltered as complete races. In his usage of them he differs in some respects from the older stories.

Fafnir, the son of Rodmar, becomes the giant Fafner, and his brother Fasolt is added. Regin is transformed into Mime, the master-smith. Instead of Otter, who must be covered by gems, we have the love goddess Friea, and instead of the hair which the Ring must cover in the old legend, it is in Wagner's adaptation one of Friea's beautiful eyes. Fafner hides in Hate Hole instead of upon Glistenheath, and is killed by Siegfried instead of Sigurd. The lonely Walküres' Rock takes the place of the house on the hill, and instead of being made invulnerable by the Dragon's blood, Siegfried is protected by Brünnhilde's spells—a fancy which seems more poetic and beautiful, but which originates, I believe, entirely with Wagner. Gutrune takes the place of Kreimhild, and Hagan is not Gunther's vassal, but his half-brother. These are, after all, apparently slight changes, yet to Wagner's cycle a new poetry seems to have come. The barbaric aspects of the tale have faded, and all the simple beauty of those wild, noble gods and demi-gods has gleamed forth as gloriously as the wonderful Rhinegold, which the master has made next in importance to the gods and the dusk of their splendor.

Before going further, perhaps it might be well to say a few words of explanation as to the motifs which form the key-notes of Wagner's great musical dramas.

When he set his poem of the Nibelungen Ring to music, he was not satisfied with merely beautiful airs and harmonies linked together with no purpose save the lovely sounds. He wished, above all, to have his music fit his words; and for every character and thought and incident, and indeed for almost everything in his operas, he wrote a melody, and these descriptive musical phrases are called _motifs_. Each one has its meaning, and when it is played it brings the thought of what it describes and represents, and it makes a double language—what the characters on the stage are saying and what the music is saying, as well. Through the motifs we understand many things which we could not possibly comprehend otherwise.

That Wagner wished to give the impression that Erda was the mother of all beings, divine and human, at the beginning of the world, he has shown by the fact that the motif of the Primal Element—the commencement of all things—is identical with hers, save that where she is indicated the melody takes a minor coloring, denoting her character of mystery as well as the gloom in which her prophetic powers must necessarily envelop her. The contrasting, yet harmonizing, elements of earth and water are also shadowed forth, I think, in this motif of the Primal Element, which is used for the *Rhine*, and also for the Goddess of the *Earth*. When the Vala's daughters—the Nornir—are mirrored in the music, the same melody appears, fraught with the waving, weaving sound of their mystic spinning.

The motifs in Wagner's operas are, above all, descriptive. For example, note the Walhalla, Nibelung, and Giant motifs.

The first of these, full of power, substance, and dignity, not only is descriptive of the great palace itself, but also represents the entire race of gods who inhabit it, seemingly secure in their conscious glory and sovereignty. To indicate Wotan, the King of the gods and the ruler in Walhalla, Wagner has constantly made use of this motif.

Its melody is measured, strong, and simple, and the nobility of those worshipped gods of primeval years seems to breathe through it.

The Nibelungs were so intimately associated with their work that they were scarcely more than living machines—soulless exponents of the art of the forge and the anvil; so when we hear in the music the beat of hammers—the sharp, metallic clang in measured time, our first thought is that the hammers are swung by the Nibelungs. How cramped is their melody, how monotonous and hopeless is the regular fall of the hammers! When we hear it hushed and veiled with discords, we seem to come in contact with the narrow, darkened souls of the Nibelungs.

And now we come to the motif of the giants.

It is, like themselves, heavy, lumbering, with a slur that is like the stumbling of heavy feet. Clumsy and ungraceful, it and what it represents cross the idyllic beauty of the motifs of Friea, Walhalla, the Ring, the Rhinegold, and the rest, with a harsh and disagreeable sense of an inharmonious element. How different from the majestic gods, and the clever, small-souled Nibelungs, are these great creatures who are all bodies and no brains, and who are so ably represented by the music allotted them in the operas! Yet, in their own way, they and their motif are extremely picturesque!

In these three motifs we can see the genius which formed them, and so many others, even greater in conception and execution. Scattered throughout *The Story of the Rhinegold* will be found a few of these motifs—only a few and not the most lovely—but enough I think to help one, in a small way, to follow the operas with more interest and understanding than if one did not know them.

One of the simplest motifs in the book is one of the most important: the Rhinegold motif. It is like the blowing of a fairy horn heralding to the world of sprites and elves the magic wonder in the river.

In the olden days they had a lovely legend of the formation of the Rhinegold. They said that the sun's rays poured down into the Rhine so brilliantly every day that, through some magic—no one knew exactly how—the glowing reflection became bright and beautiful gold, filled with great mystic powers because of its glorious origin—the sunshine.

And that was the beginning of the Rhinegold.

A. A. C.

# CONTENTS

## Part IV

## THE DUSK OF THE GODS, or *GÖTTER-DÄMMERUNG*

# ILLUSTRATIONS

# Part I

# THE RHINEGOLD, OR *DAS RHEINGOLD*

Motif of the Rhinegold

# PRELUDE

WE have, all of us, read of the Golden Age,
when the gods ruled over the world, and giants
and dragons, dwarfs and water-fairies inhabited
the earth and mingled with mortals. The giants
were then a strong, stupid race, more rough than
cruel, and, as a rule, generous among themselves.
They were very foolish creatures, and constantly
did themselves and others harm ; but their race,
even at that time, was dying out, and there were
left of it only two brothers, Fasolt and Fafner.

The dwarfs, or Nibelungs, were entirely different. They were small and misshapen, but very
shrewd, and so skilful were their fingers that
they were able to do the most difficult work in
the finest metals. They lived in an underground
country called Nibelheim (Home of the Dwarfs),
where they collected hoards of gold and gems,
and strange treasures of all kinds ; and Alberich
was one of them. He was a hideous creature,

so dark and evil-looking, with his small, wicked eyes and his hair and beard the color of ink, that he was always called Black Alberich — a very suitable name.

As for the dragons, they were rare even in those days, and though we shall have to deal with one by-and-by when we are further on in my story, I shall not say much about them now.

The water-fairies were beautiful spirits who lived in the depths of the river Rhine. They were simple and innocent, as became children of the Golden Age, and very lovely to look upon. In the peaceful twilight-land under the water they were perfectly happy, dancing in and out among the rocks at the river bottom, and singing soft songs, which, when wafted up to the surface of the Rhine, sounded like the faint sighing ripple of the river as it rolled onward through the valleys and the woods.

And the water-fairies had one great happiness in their quiet, shadowed lives. I will tell you what it was: On the top of a tall black rock in the river Rhine there rested a magical treasure, more wonderful than any of the Nibelung hoards, or the possessions of the gods themselves—a bright, beautiful Gold, the radiance of which was so great that when the sun shone down into the river and touched it the gray-green water was filled with golden light from depth to depth, and the fairies of the Rhine circled about their treasure, singing and laughing with delight.

What a wonderful time it must have been—the Golden Age—when such things were possible!

You smile and say that they were not possible, even then! Remember that this is a fairy tale— a day-dream—such as might come to you while watching the sunlit ripples dancing on the water, and hearing the little waves lapping on the pebbles—a fairy tale, that is all.

The Golden Age, as I think of it, seems a period in which anything might have happened. Closing my eyes, I can picture the majestic gods moving, great kings and queens among human beings; great kings and queens made young by Friea's apples of youth. Friea was the Goddess of Love, Youth, and Beauty. She was the same as Venus, the Roman goddess, called Aphrodite by the Greeks, of whom, perhaps, you have read elsewhere. All that I am writing about happened, you know, in Germany; and to the people there the gods—or rather men's ideas of them, and their names for them—were different from those of other lands.

So the King God, instead of being Jupiter, or

Zeus, or Jove, was called Wotan, or sometimes Odin. And the Queen Goddess was neither Juno nor Here, but Fricka; and the wild Thunder God was Thor; and the Goddess of the Earth Erda, which means the earth. She was the wisest of all the gods and goddesses (though Logi, the Fire God, was the quickest and cleverest), and she could prophesy strange things about the gods and the world, and everything happened just as she prophesied.

She would sink into the earth and dream, and all her dreams came true. She would tell them to her daughters, the three Norns, or Fates, and they would weave them into a long golden thread, into which they had spun the world's history.

They spun under a great ash-tree which grew by the Fountain of Wisdom, and was called the Tree of the World.

One day Wotan, the king of the gods, came to the fountain for a draught of the Water of Wisdom. He drank, and left one of his eyes in payment. He tore a limb from the World-Ash and made it into a spear; and the spear, having strange figures upon it representing Law and Knowledge, was typical of the wisdom and power of the gods, and so long as that wisdom and that power endured no sword could break the spear nor could remain whole at its touch.

But the World - Ash, robbed of its branches, withered away and died, and the Fountain of Wisdom became dry.

And these things were the beginning of the end of the Golden Age. But wise people say that the Golden Age did not end until men began to value gold for its own sake and the love of gain, and to do wrong things to possess it. And now I will tell you how it all happened.

Motif of the Primal Element,

out of which come the Erda, Norn, and Rhine Motifs

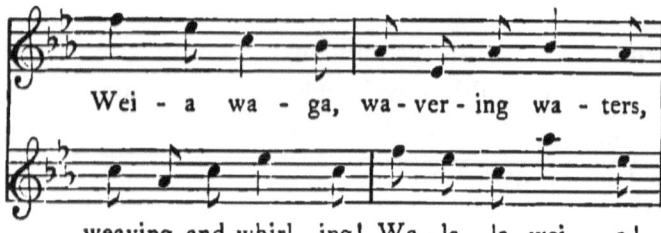

Wei - a wa - ga, wa-ver-ing wa - ters,

weaving and whirl- ing! Wa-la-la wei - a!

## CHAPTER I

### THE RHINE MAIDENS

AT the bottom of the river Rhine, about the dark rock where rested the invisible Rhinegold, there swam one morning before sunrise the Gold's fair guardians, the three children of the Rhine. They were beautiful maidens, these three water-spirits, the most lovely of all the river people, and their names were Flosshilde, Woglinde, and Wellgunde. They were singing softly, and glancing constantly up to the rock's crest, waiting for the appearance of the Rhinegold, which could only be seen when the sun had risen up above and sent its rays into the water to disclose the treasure. They sang a little rippling refrain that meant nothing except laughter and joy, and sounded very like the ripples of the water themselves:

"Weia waga—"

sang Woglinde,

"Wavering waters, weaving and whirling,
Walala weia!"

And so they sang on, till their voices mingled so with the ripple that both voices and water became almost one in sound.

Now, while these three lovely maids, seeming almost part of the water in their dresses of shimmering blue - green, with pale wreaths of river flowers in their hair, and their white arms looking frail as moonbeams as they raised them through the water—while they moved about the rock singing and laughing together, a strange, dark little man stood near watching them. He had risen out of a black chasm in one of the rocks, and he had come from far Nibelheim, through an underground passage. He had small eyes, his hair and beard were the color of ink, and he looked very wicked. Can you guess who he was?

He shouted gruffly to the Rhine Maidens, and they, being much amused at his ugly appearance, drew near with laughter and mocking words. They led him wild chases in among the rocks, they played with him merry games of hide-and-seek—merry for them, but not at all so for him, for he was clumsy in motion compared with them, and he became very angry because he could not follow them over the rocks.

"Smooth, slippery, slush and slime," he grumbled. "The dampness makes me sneeze."

At last, just as he had become thoroughly angry, there appeared suddenly a strange brightness at the top of the rock—a wonderful golden light that glowed with ever-increasing brilliance down into the water.

"Ah, see, sisters!" cried Woglinde. "The awakening sun laughs down into the depths."

"Yes," said Wellgunde, with soft delight, "it greets the slumbering Gold!"

"With a kiss of light the Gold is aroused!" said Flosshilde. And, joining hands, they swam excitedly about the rock, singing in bursts of gladness:

> " Weia waga,
>   Weia waga,
>   Rhinegold, Rhinegold,
>   Glorious joy."

"You gliders," questioned Alberich (for it was

THE GLEAMING TREASURE

he), "what is this that gleams and glistens over yonder?"

Laughing at his ignorance, the nymphs told him that it was a magical Gold; that whoever made a Ring from it would have greater power than any one else alive; that he could possess all the wealth of the world if he wished; and they so described the fairy powers of the treasure that Alberich's wicked soul began to thrill with desire to have it as his own.

The sisters further told him that the Gold was safe from thieves, because it could only be stolen by some one who had made up his mind never to love any one except himself so long as he might live.

"We have nothing to fear," said gentle Woglinde, "for every one who lives must love."

But Alberich pondered silently. "All the wealth in the world!" he thought. "For that who would not give up love?" And he sprang wildly up the rocks.

"Listen, waves and water-witches!" he shouted, as he reached towards the gleaming treasure. "Never will I, the Dwarf, give love to any creature save myself through all my life." And while, with wild cries, the Rhine Maidens hastened near to prevent him, Alberich, the Nibelung, tore the

Rhinegold from the tall, black rock, and fled with it into the black chasm, and so to Nibelheim.

And, left behind, the nymphs could only wail for their lost joy with sobs and cries of " Sorrow, sorrow!   Ah—to rescue the Gold !"

But it was too late.   And in the dark hollow chasm, Alberich, fleeing with the treasure, laughed at their despair.

Motif of the Giants

Motif of Friea

## CHAPTER II

### FASOLT AND FAFNER

ONE morning not long afterwards the rising sun shone upon strange things up among the gods.

Wotan, and Fricka his wife, waking upon the mountain-top where they had slept that night, gazed up to where, built among the clouds, the spires of a wonderful palace glittered in the sun-shine—Walhalla, the fair, new home of the gods.

It had been built at Wotan's command by Fasolt and Fafner, the two brother giants, and they had been promised, in payment, the goddess Friea. But Wotan had never intended giving her to them, and so he told Fricka when she spoke anxiously of the reward promised the giants, declaring that the goddess was as precious to him as to her.

Even as he spoke Friea rushed wildly in, calling upon him to save her from the rude giants. In answer, Wotan asked where Logi, the Fire God, could be found, saying that where cunning and craft were needed, Logi was the one most to be sought after. But, look as he might, the wayward Fire God was nowhere to be seen.

And then came the great brothers, bearing huge clubs, and fiercely clamoring for a reward for their labors in building Walhalla.

" You slept while we worked," they said. " Now claim we our payment."

" What price do you demand?" asked Wotan, pretending not to remember any promised reward. " What will you take as wages?"

" Would you deceive us so?" cried Fasolt, in

astonished rage. "Friea you promised us. We worked right heartily to win us so fair a woman."

"Hush!" muttered Fafner. "Listen to me! Without Friea's apples of youth the gods will grow old, and their glory will fade away. They will die like human beings if Friea be taken from them."

So the giants talked together, planning how to steal the lovely goddess, who stood aside trembling, fearing that Wotan would refuse to protect her from the two savage workmen.

He meanwhile merely murmured softly to himself, "Logi is long coming," and gazed expectantly about. But still the Fire God could not be seen.

Thor and Froh, two other gods, had appeared. The giants were growing more impatient and Friea more despairing, when Logi at last arrived. When he did he talked on a variety of subjects before he would pay any attention to the affairs that were worrying the other gods and the giants. But at last he set his clever brain to work at some plan by which his fair sister Friea might be saved. Knowing well the love of wealth characteristic of the giants, he told the story of the Rhinegold and the stealing of it by the Nibelung. He said that he had heard the maids weeping for their lost treasure, and had promised them that Wotan, the King God, would return it to them in time. The two giants began to feel the same desire for it that Alberich had had, and to whisper together concerning it, so vividly did Logi describe its powers.

" It seems," muttered Fafner, " that this Gold is worth even more than Friea." And he cried out suddenly: " Listen, Wotan, you wise one! We will give up Friea; but you will instead bestow upon us the Nibelung's Gold."

" We will hold her meanwhile as ransom!" cried Fasolt. And they dragged her away, despite her piteous appeals, to Riesenheim (or Home of the Giants), leaving the gods perplexed and sorrowing for their lost goddess.

As they stood silently together a mist seemed to steal upward from the ground, and floated between them. A strange shadow rested upon the faces of the gods. They looked pale and wrinkled; their hair was white.

" Alas! What has happened?" wailed Fricka, faintly.

The gods were growing old.

" See, then," said Logi, the shrewd one. " Our Youth Goddess has gone. We are old; we are gray. The race of gods will come to an end."

Wotan started and looked about him. His face was pale.

" Down, Logi ! Let us go down to Nibelheim !" he cried. " The Gold shall be had for ransom."

The gods called out good wishes after them through the mist, and Wotan, the King God, and his fire - servant, Logi, went down through the hollow, shadowy passages under the earth to Nibelheim, the home of the dwarfs.

Ring Motif

Nibelung Motif

## CHAPTER III

### NIBELHEIM

ALBERICH had forged a Ring from the Rhine-gold, and, wearing it, possessed absolute power over the rest of the Nibelungs. He was the King Dwarf, ruler over all Nibelheim, the Land of Gloom. Ah! what a land of gloom it was! Through the dark shadows there streamed fitfully a lurid light from the forges where the dwarfs were working; their hammers clanged monotonously on the anvils. Slowly they laid the results of their toil in great heaps, and Alberich laughed at their weariness and gloated over the treasures, which he promptly claimed as his own.

Among the Nibelungs was one particularly

crooked and ill-shapen, named Mime. He was Alberich's half-brother, and, not unnaturally, hated the Black King with all his strength; for Alberich treated him even more cruelly than the others.

Mime, at Alberich's command, made a wonderful cap of darkness out of some of the Rhinegold, which not only had the power of making its wearer invisible at will, but could change him into whatever shape he wished. This Alberich wore, and changed himself into a column of mist, in which shape he found he could move about much faster, and make things much harder for the dwarfs.

"Hohei, all you Nibelungs! Kneel to your King! Now he is everywhere, all about you, unseen, but felt and heard, you idlers!"

And the column of mist drifted off through a rocky passage, leaving Mime whimpering upon the ground.

Now, with the clang of the hammers there mingled the sound of steps, and from the black crevice in the rocks came two figures slowly down to Nibelheim. One was tall and majestic, with a helmet of gold and steel, a long cloak with strange designs upon it, and a deep golden beard that hung far down over his breast; one

of his eyes was missing, and in his hand he bore
a great spear.

The other was clothed in brilliant red, his eyes
were bright, his step swift as a springing flame in
dead grass. They were Wotan and Logi search-
ing for the Rhinegold.

Logi accosted Mime in friendly fashion, and
asked what was wrong with him.

"That wretch, my brother!" grumbled the
Dwarf. "He treats us all cruelly. Leave me
in peace!"

"How came Alberich by his power?" asked
the Fire God.

"From the ruddy Rhinegold he made a Ring.
With it he rules us. But," asked the Nibelung,
staring at them, "who are you both?"

"Friends that perhaps may free the Nibelung people," laughed Logi, and at the same time
Alberich appeared, scolding, screaming, and ill-
treating all who came in his way. Driving Mime
away with the rest of the dwarfs, he, scowling,
asked the two gods what they wished.

"We heard of the wonders worked by Alberich," answered Wotan. "We come to behold
them."

"Pooh! I know you well," said the Dwarf
King. "Such notable guests"—and he sneered

—"could only have been led by envy to Nibelheim."

"Surely you know me," said Logi. "I have
lit your forges, gnome. Cannot you trust me?"

"To be sure I know you," grinned Alberich.
"And I will always trust you to be untrustwor-
thy. I don't fear you."

"How brave you are," said Logi, in pretended
admiration.

"Do you see that treasure?" said the Nibelung, proudly pointing to a great heap of gold
and gems.

The gods assented.

"But," said Wotan, "what good does it do
you, here in Nibelheim?"

Alberich glared at him, and then laughed.

"Ha! ha! But wait!" he said. "You gods!
You gods! You have looked down upon us
Nibelungs. Now we, with the help of the Gold-
en Ring, will sway the whole world. We will
storm the gates of Walhalla! Beware! Ha!
ha! Do you hear me? Beware!"

Wotan, in anger, started forward, but Logi
slipped in front of him.

"Most wonderful are you, O Nibelung!" he
said, admiringly. "I salute you as the might-
iest creature alive. But tell me one thing, O

wise one.   How guard you your Ring from thieves?"

"Does Logi think that all are as foolish as himself?" asked Alberich.   "That danger I provided for.   A Cap of Darkness, called the Tarnhelm, is mine, to change me into whatever shape I wish, and also to hide me at any time.   So, my friend, guard I my Ring, sleeping or waking, as I wish."

"Wondrous above all it seems!" cried Logi. "Prove it, O Dwarf!"

"That I will.   What shape shall I take?"

"Whatever you wish," answered Logi.   "It is sure to be wonderful."

Alberich placed the metal cap upon his head and became a great dragon, writhing on the ground.

"Wonderful!" cried the gods.

"Yet I should again like to behold its ·magic. Is it possible to become small as well as large by its aid?" asked Logi.   "I beg of you show us if you can become small, O great one!"

"Nothing easier!" cried Alberich, beginning to enjoy himself.   "Look, then, O gods!"   He placed the helmet on his head and vanished.   A toad hopped on the ground in his stead.

"Quick!   Hold him!" cried the Fire God;

and Wotan firmly held the toad with his foot, while Logi lifted up the Tarnhelm, which still rested upon its great head. And behold! Alberich lay at their feet, struggling and roaring with rage.

The Fire God produced a rope, and the two gods bound the Nibelung and carried him with them, up the dark passage-way through which they had descended, and left behind them the crimson fires, the clanging hammers, the gloom, and hopelessness of Nibelheim.

Motif of Alberich's Spell

## CHAPTER IV

### THE RAINBOW BRIDGE

OUT of the underground world into the wild, mountainous country above, veiled still with the strange gray mist of age, came the two gods and their captive, Alberich.

He was snarling and grumbling, being much enraged at being bound by the hated gods, and, above all, at having his beloved Tarnhelm in the hands of Logi, whom he especially detested. Also, he feared that he would be forced to give up the Ring, which he still wore on his finger ; and, partly to prevent the gods from wishing for this, he soon consented to give them the hoard which his servants, the Nibelungs, had collected in Nibelheim. Touching the Ring with his lips, he murmured a command, or spell, and from the under - world came the little dark dwarfs bearing great loads of treasure, which they placed at his feet.

Ashamed, and hating that they should see him
a captive, Alberich loudly ordered them off with
threats and harsh words, and then demanded that
the gods should release him, while the Nibelungs
crept back into the dark hole that led to Nibelheim.

Logi, casting the Tarnhelm upon the pile, asked
if the Dwarf should be freed.

" He wears a bright Ring," said the King God.
" Let it be added to the heap!"

" The Ring!" wildly cried Alberich. " The
Ring! I will never give it up! It is mine!"

" Thief! You stole it from the Rhine Children," said Wotan. " Do you call it, then,
yours?" and he tore the Ring from Alberich's
finger and placed it on his own.

"Let him go!" he said to Logi, who obeyed,"
and the Nibelung was free. Rising from the
ground, he glared horribly at the gods.

" Listen to the spell I cast on the Ring!" he
said, with a peal of wild laughter. " None who
possess it shall ever through it come to happiness. Sorrow attends it, and whoever owns it
shall know grief. His death shall be sad, his life
a failure. This doom shall attend the Ring until
it comes back to my hand. Hear the spell Alberich has placed on the Gold!"

He laughed again, and vanished in the dark hole that led to Nibelheim.

Wotan stood silently gazing at the Ring on his finger. Logi, looking off in the distance, saw Fasolt and Fafner nearing, with Friea. As she came closer, the gray mist began to clear slightly away, though it still hung about in heavy clouds, hiding Walhalla's spires. Fricka, Thor, and Froh, quickly drawing near from another direction, spoke of the growing warmth and clearness of the air.

"Dear sister, welcome back to us!" cried Fricka, as the giants strode out with Friea. But, when the two goddesses started forward to meet each other, Fasolt caught hold of his captive and held her fast.

"Wait! Wait!" he cried. "Where is the ransom?"

"Behold it!" said Wotan, pointing to the heap of treasure.

The giants declared that when a pile of gold had been erected high enough to hide the Love Goddess from view, they would return her to the gods—but not before. Accordingly, a heap was made which, as it grew higher with added treasure, soon hid Friea entirely, save for a gleam of her bright hair, which Fafner's keen eye descried. The Tarnhelm must go to hide it.

That accomplished, Fasolt strained his eyes to find an unfilled crevice. Through a tiny space he beheld one of the goddess's eyes, and demanded the Ring to fill up the chink.

" The Ring !" exclaimed Wotan, starting back.

"The Ring !" cried Logi. " Nonsense ! It is the Rhine Children's treasure. The King God will return it to them."

" Foolish you are," said Wotan, in a low voice. " I shall keep it myself."

" Bad is the prospect for the fulfilment of my promise to the weeping Rhine Children," said Logi, softly.

"Your promise does not bind me," said the King of the Gods. " I shall keep the Ring."

" Hand over the ransom !" cried Fafner, loudly.

" Never !" said Wotan.

" Then Friea is ours !" roared the giants, and they grasped her once more.

The gods, in chorus, begged Wotan to give the wranglers the treasure, but he was deaf to their entreaties. His eyes were fastened upon the bright Ring's glitter ; he was blind to all else.

Suddenly the light seemed to die out from the world. All grew dark. From a black chasm in the rocks rose a woman's figure in a strange halo of blue light. Her face was pale, with a look of deepest mystery upon it. Lifting her hand, she spoke in low, solemn tones to Wotan:

" Hear my warning! Avoid the Ring, with its terrible spell! Heed me, O Wotan!"

" Who are you who warn me?" asked the god.

" I understand all things; wisest in all the world am I. The witch-wife Erda, men call me, Mother of the Norns. Listen, listen, listen! A day of dusk and gloom is coming for the gods. Beware of the Ring!"

She sank down into the earth once more. The blue light faded away. As she vanished she spoke again:

" Think well on what I have said!"

She was gone. Slowly the light came back to the world. Lost in thought, Wotan stood a moment; then turned quickly to the giants, and tore the Ring from his finger.

" It is yours!" he declared; and he tossed it on to the pile. " Back to us, Friea!" and the Love Goddess gladly flew back to their midst.

Fafner and Fasolt began fighting over the Ring at once, and Alberich's dark spell quickly made itself felt. For Fasolt, seizing the Ring, was killed by his brother, who, with Ring and treasure, fled away to a far cave, named Hate Hole, and there, in the shape of a great dragon, guarded his hoard in loneliness for many years. But that is a different part of my story.

After the death of Fasolt and the flight of Fafner with the treasure, the clouds hanging low over the gods were cleared away by a great storm, and, as Walhalla appeared shining in the sun, a rainbow bridge spanned the space between the palace and the gods, who passed over it to their new home.

"These gods — how foolish and blind!" said Logi to himself, as he went with them. "I feel ashamed that I am one of them, bound to share in their doings."

The beautiful palace glittered brightly. The gods smiled as they passed over the rainbow bridge. Only from the Rhine below there came a sound of wailing.

"O Rhinegold! Rhinegold!" sang the weeping Rhine daughters. "We long for your light. Trustful are those in the water; false are those above."

Walhalla Motif

# Part II

# THE WARRIOR GODDESS, OR *DIE WALKÜRE*

Storm Motif

# PRELUDE

I SHALL now take a long leap in my story, going on to a time when the gods had been happy in Walhalla for many years. Wotan alone felt dreary forebodings, though, as yet, there were no real signs of any downfall of the gods. So heavy were these presentiments that he began to fill his halls with heroes able to defend Walhalla, if Alberich should ever regain the Ring, and, keeping his word, storm the gates of the gods' palace. At Wotan's command, his nine daughters, the Walküres (or Warrior Goddesses) watched over all combats between heroes, carrying those who were killed to Walhalla, where Friea's smiles brought them to life again.

And this was not the only strange thing that had come to pass since the gods had entered their new palace.

Among Wotan's descendants were a race of people called the Volsungs, and at the time of

3

which I am writing only two of them were alive, a boy and a girl, who had been brought up from babyhood almost like brother and sister, and who were very much alike, having the golden hair of their ancestor Wotan, and eyes in which there was a curious glitter, as bright as that of the snake's glance.

Both were as beautiful as the sun, like all the Volsungs; both were strong and warm-hearted and noble, and they loved each other as much as though they had been really brother and sister.

While still very young, they became separated for years; for, while the boy was out hunting, the girl, Sieglinde, was stolen away by a robber named Hunding. She led a dreary life as the Robber's servant, until she became a woman. But she always felt confident that help would come to her in time, because one night, at a feast given by Hunding, a stranger had entered, robed in the rough garb of a wanderer, but with kingly bearing. One of his eyes was missing. He had struck a sword into the trunk of a great tree which grew up from the centre of Hunding's house, declaring that whoever could draw it out should have it for his own. And all had tried their best, but the blade would not yield an inch.

A WARRIOR GODDESS

Then the Wanderer had laughed and depart-
ed. But Sieglinde, thinking of it dreamily, remembered that, while he had frowned on the
others, he had looked kindly on her ; and, gazing at the sword, she began to feel, after a while,
that whoever could pull it forth would be her
rescuer. And so the years passed.

She did not know that the Wanderer had
been none other than the first father of all
the race of Volsungs—Wotan, the king of the
gods.

Siegmund, the boy, as he grew to manhood,
became a very wolf in wildness, but a great warrior, and a stanch hero. He led a roving life,
with few friends, and, alas ! many enemies. His
generous heart brought him into sad dilemmas
sometimes; as, for instance, when, at a maid-
en's request, he defended her from her relations,
who wished to marry her to some one whom she
hated. When, in doing battle for her, he killed
one of her kinsmen, she had flung herself upon
the dead man and accused her defender of
cruelty.

He fought the rude warriors who were pressing up about her until his weapons were torn
from him, and he was driven away into the
woods through a wild storm which seemed to

blow him on with irresistible violence, until he found himself at the door of a house.

Utterly exhausted, he staggered in, filled only with the desire to rest and shelter his tired body from the storm. And the house was that of Hunding, the Robber.

Hunding Motif

Volsung Motif

## CHAPTER I

### THE HOUSE OF HUNDING

OUTSIDE the storm was raging, the great pines were bending in the wild gale, the thunder and lightning were in mad commotion.

Inside, rude as the hut was, there were warmth and apparent peace. A large fire burned on the hearth, and sent its fitful glare from time to time flashing about the bare hall ; now shining on the sword-hilt in the great oak-tree growing in the centre ; now lighting the dark corners with a faint red gleam. A heap of skins was beside the hearth, and upon this Siegmund sank exhausted.

As he lay there the door opened, and Sieglinde came quickly from an inner room. Frightened by the sight of a stranger, she accosted him in trembling tones. Receiving no answer, she came nearer, and, looking down at him, she saw a strong, tall man, with golden hair, and a face as beautiful as the sun. Caught over his shoulder was a great black bear-skin, and his face was like that of a king among men. His eyes were closed as she bent over him; but, after a moment or two, he opened them and gasped faintly, "Water! Water!" only to sink back once more, exhausted, as Sieglinde hastened away to draw him a draught at the spring. She was soon back with what he had asked for, and, giving it, looked down kindly as he drank.

When he had finished, he gazed up at her and saw a beautiful maiden, with the rough, gray skin of some wild animal worn loosely over her long white robe. She had hair of as deep a gold as his own, and a face full of sweetness and a sympathy that he had never known before.

Rising from the hearth, he gently wished her good fortune, and thanked her for her kindness to a friendless man, who must now pass on his way lest the sorrow which followed his footsteps should come to her; and, so saying, was about to leave the house when Sieglinde, who

in some way felt that this man was to be her
rescuer, sprang forward and begged him to stay,
saying that as sorrow had dwelt in the house for
many days she did not fear its coming. So he
consented to remain until Hunding, who was out
hunting, should return.

Going back to the hearth, he stood there
quietly looking, in a long silence, towards Sieglinde, and both felt, I think, that it was Fate
that he, and none other, should stay and rescue
her. So they stood silently waiting for the Robber's return, and the fire crackled and glowed
and flickered about the hall.

Suddenly, Sieglinde started; for the sound of
hoofs broke the stillness, and they could hear
the Robber leading his horse to the stable. Almost directly afterwards the door opened, and
Hunding himself came in. He was not a pleas-
ant-looking creature, for he was very tall and
very broad-shouldered, and as wild in appearance as a wolf, and his face was dark and angry.
His long hair and beard were black and tangled, his eyes were fierce, and he wore queer,
jangling armor and bands of steel on his bare
arms.

He stopped short, and sternly pointed to the
stranger, glaring at Sieglinde in great anger.

Reading a fierce question in his look, she answered, quietly:

"I found this man weary upon the hearth. Need drove him into the house."

Hunding relented a little; and, after handing her his shield and weapons, said quietly to Siegmund:

"Safe is my hearth! Safe for you is my house!" Then, turning to Sieglinde, he roughly bade her hasten with the supper. She bore away the heavy weapons and rested them against the tree in the centre of the hall; then went about arranging the evening meal. As they sat down on the rough seats around the scantily spread table, Hunding asked his guest his name, and whence he had come on so stormy a night. Sieglinde leaned eagerly forward as the warrior began his tale.

He told them the story of his life, only calling himself Woful the Wolfing instead of Siegmund the Volsung. And when he came to the tale of the maiden and her kinsmen, and of how he had killed one of them, and fought the others until he was disarmed and driven into the forest, Hunding rose in great anger and stood looking at his guest with wrath in his eyes.

"You win every one's hate," he declared.

"My friends sent for me to help them revenge the shedding of blood. I went to their aid, but it was too late. Now, when I return, I find the enemy himself upon my hearth. They were my friends against whom you fought; and, though to-night custom makes you safe as a guest in my house, to-morrow you shall die, Wolfing! So be prepared!"

So both the Robber and his servant, the maiden Sieglinde, went away, leaving Siegmund alone by the hearth, sad and a little perplexed. For Sieglinde, as she left the hall, had pointed swiftly towards the sword-hilt buried in the tree. The fire leaped up wildly as he stood gazing towards the oak, and the light touched the bright hilt and painted it red for a moment, then died once more. Siegmund dreamily wondered if the light on the steel had been left by the glance Sieglinde had cast towards it. For you see he had fallen in love with this lovely woman, who looked at him so kindly, and whose face was as fair and beautiful as the sun.

The gold and rosy flashes from the fire grew fainter, the shadows deepened, and Siegmund fell asleep.

Now perhaps you wonder why he stayed there instead of going out into the night, where he would be safe. There were three good reasons to keep him.

In the first place, he was too brave a hero to fly from danger; and, in the second place, he did not want to leave the beautiful maiden alone in the Robber's power; and the third reason was as good a one as either of the others. Hunding had said: "Custom makes you safe as a guest in my house," which meant that it would be both unfair and wrong if he, Hunding, killed a stranger taking shelter under his roof. This was called the Law of Hospitality, and the law was never taken advantage of by any honorable guest. So, if Siegmund had run away after Hunding had so well observed the Law of Hospitality he would have been dishonorable as well as cowardly, and it was just as though he had given a promise that he would not go away that night.

In the meantime Siegmund lay asleep. From an inner room came the beautiful maiden swiftly to his side. Awaking him, she told him to hurry away while there was yet time. She said that she had sprinkled some sleep spices into Hunding's wine, and that he would slumber soundly and long; and she begged the guest to go away quietly into the night and save himself.

Finally, she told him of the Wanderer who had come and struck the sword into the oak-tree, and told him, too, how she had waited in vain for some hero who would draw forth the sword and rescue her.

Siegmund said that he would claim the sword for his own, and drag it from the tree, and, as he spoke, the door opened wide. Perhaps the good fairies unlatched it. Without, it was very still; the storm had ceased, and the moon was shining wondrously.

Then Sieglinde, looking in his face, seemed to see there a resemblance to some one she had known long ago, and, gazing into his eyes, she asked him if he were really a Wolfing.

" No, a Volsung !" replied the hero, proudly. And she cried out in joy: "A Volsung! Are you, too, a Volsung — one of my race? It was for you, indeed, that the Wanderer struck the sword into the oak."

Springing to the tree, Siegmund laid his hand on the hilt and broke into a wild chant, naming the sword which he had come to, when in such pressing need, Nothung (or Needful).

With a mighty wrench he drew it out of the oak's trunk, and held it above his head.

"I am Siegmund the Volsung!" he shouted, exultantly.

Then he asked her more gently if she would follow him away from the house of the enemy Hunding, telling her that if she would be his wife he would defend her with Nothung, and make her life one long spring-tide.

"As you are Siegmund, I am Sieglinde!" cried she, aloud. "It is right that the Volsungs should become joined as one."

And into the night they went away together; for the storm had ceased and the brightness of the moonlight was most marvellous.

Sword Motif

Brünnhilde's Call

" Ho - yo - to - ho . . . . . !"

Motif of the Volsung's heroism

## CHAPTER II

### THE DAUGHTER OF WOTAN

UP in the mountains near a rocky gorge, where the wind swept and the wild pines grew, stood Wotan, king of the gods, and before him, awaiting his orders, was his favorite daughter, Brünnhilde, the Walküre.

She was very beautiful, more beautiful than any woman who ever breathed. Her hair was golden bright, her figure queenly. When she moved, the motion of a bird was not more fleet and graceful, and her face was what you might suppose the face of a goddess would be. She wore long white robes and glistening armor, and the wings in her bright helmet were like snow. She bore a spear and shield also, for you know she was a goddess of war, and, as her business was to attend the battles of heroes, she arrayed herself accordingly.

She moved restlessly, and seemed anxious to be off, for at the top of a rocky slope was not her horse, Grani, waiting for her to spring on his back and gallop away through the clouds?

Wotan, whom, of course, you remember, stood leaning on his spear. He looked for the moment glad, for he was very fond of his descendants, the Volsungs, and he also believed that Siegmund would one day kill Fafner, the Dragon, with the sword which had been placed in the oak for the purpose, and would return to the Rhine Maidens their treasure. When this should come to pass, the gods would have no more fear of Alberich.

When Wotan thought of all these possibilities, the dusk of the gods' bright day seemed far off. So it was with a thrill of joy in his voice that he spoke to Brünnhilde, and bade her make ready to attend the fight between Siegmund and Hunding, which, as the Robber was already hunting for his guest with fierce hounds, was sure to occur that day.

"Aid the Volsung, my brave maiden!" said the King God. " Overthrow Hunding! Hasten tò the battle!"

" Hoyotoho!" shouted the Walküre, waving her spear as she sprang up the rocks. " Hoyotoho! Hoyotoho!"

On a high pinnacle of boulders she paused, and looked down on Wotan once more. "Look well, father! Here comes Fricka. I leave you to her."

With a clear burst of laughter she sped on again. Her boisterous " Hoyotoho!" died away among the echoes.

In a golden car, drawn by two rams, came Fricka, the queen of the gods. She seemed in great haste, and, springing to the ground, stood in all her majesty before the King God, with anger in her eyes.

" I ask for right!" she began, drawing her scarlet draperies about her. And she went on to demand vengeance for Hunding; vengeance upon Siegmund, the guest, for having taken advantage of the host who had observed so well the Law of Hospitality; vengeance upon him who, from the house of Hunding, had stolen the Robber's servant, Sieglinde.

All this made Wotan very unhappy, for he

loved Siegmund, and already in his heart had
forgiven him for what he had done.   Yet he
knew that all wrong must bring punishment,
and asked Fricka what she wished him to do.

" Call back the Walküre !" said the Queen
Goddess, and there was a look of triumph on
her face.   " Break the Volsung's sword !   Promise me !"

There was a pause.

" I—promise," said the god, covering his face
with his hands.

Triumphant and satisfied, Fricka drove away,
and, as she went, Brünnhilde, who had returned
while the King and Queen were talking together,
and had led her horse into a cave near by, came
to her father, asking why he seemed so sorrowful.

Tenderly drawing her to him, he told her the
story you know so well, of the stealing of the
Gold, the building of Walhalla, and the prophecy
of Erda.   He told her of the day of which the
Earth Witch had spoken, when the world would
be in twilight and gloom—the Dusk of the Gods.

He told her, too, the hopes he had had of the
great deeds to be done by Siegmund.   He let
her see how it filled him with the deepest sorrow
to overthrow the Volsung.   But the Volsung had

taken advantage of the Law of Hospitality, and Wotan had promised that he would overthrow him; and the promise must be kept. He bade her vanquish Siegmund in the coming battle and give the victory to Hunding; then, heart-broken, he wended his way among the rocks, and was gone.

Sadly Brünnhilde gazed after him. Her heart, too, was aching, because, though she loved to carry heroes to Walhalla, she loved still more to aid them in battle. She went slowly into the cave.

It was growing darker. Now, from out the gloom that filled the rocky gorge came Siegmund and his beautiful wife, Sieglinde, seeking rest in a sheltered place. Sieglinde was almost exhausted, for the way they had come was long and hard; and, after trying vainly to make her tired limbs carry her farther, she fainted at the young Volsung's feet. Tenderly he carried her to a rock near by, and, seating himself upon it, gently supported her and stooped down to listen to her breathing.

As he raised his head, satisfied that she still lived, a grave, sweet voice sounded on his ear. He turned his eyes to where stood a beautiful woman in white and steel, one arm on the neck

4

of her horse. It was the Walküre, who, according to her custom, came to warn the man who was shortly to be killed in battle. It grew still darker.

"Siegmund," said the Walküre, "look on me! Soon you must follow me!"

Siegmund, wondering, asked who she was.

"Only those who are shortly to die may see my face," answered Brünnhilde. "I bear them away to Wotan, in Walhalla. There you will find innumerable heroes who have died in battle. They will welcome you."

Siegmund asked if his father, Volse, were among the heroes.

Brünnhilde answered "Yes."

Quietly the young warrior asked if his beautiful bride might accompany him.

The Walküre slowly shook her head.

"Lonely upon the earth she remains," she answered. "Siegmund will see Sieglinde no more."

"Then greet Walhalla and the heroes for me," said the Volsung; "for there I will follow you not."

"You have looked on the face of the Walküre," said Brünnhilde. "You must die."

And, by degrees, she made him understand

THE WALKÜRE APPEARS

that death was awaiting him, that he was doomed to be killed by Hunding. In despair Siegmund raised Nothung, the sword, and declared that he would kill his wife and himself, so that they might be together in death. But Brünnhilde, who had felt her heart grow more and more tender towards this unhappy pair, started forward, bidding him hope, and declared that she would help him, instead of Hunding, in the combat, and save both himself and his wife.

" I shall be with you in battle," she promised; and she hurried away, leading her horse.

It grew darker and darker. Storm-clouds were gathering, and the rocky gorge was filled with a dense, black shadow. In the distance came the sound of Hunding's horn. Waving his sword, Siegmund sprang up the rocks to meet the enemy.

Sieglinde, dreaming softly where her husband had left her, was awakened by a wild burst of thunder and lightning. She started up frantically, trying to see through the darkness. Clouds were all about her, veiling the rocks on every side. Hunding's deep horn-call sounded nearer and nearer. Finally, from a high rock among the trees on the top of a wooded slope she could hear the voices of the combatants and the clash of weapons. Suddenly, in a vivid glare of lightning, Brünnhilde appeared among the clouds, stooping low over Siegmund, and protecting him with outstretched shield. Clear and strong rang out her voice over the tumult:

"Be firm, Siegmund! Strike quickly."

But now Sieglinde, staring wildly up through the darkness, paralyzed with fright, saw a fierce crimson light — the light that heralded the approach of the angry King God — and Wotan stood revealed in the clouds above Hunding.

"Away from my spear!" he cried, in a terrible voice. "Let the sword be splintered!" And he stretched out his weapon, made from the World-Ash. Nothung was shivered in pieces upon it, and the Robber Hunding, with one blow killed Siegmund, the Volsung.

With a great cry Sieglinde sank to the ground, but through the cloudy darkness came Brünnhilde. She lifted the poor woman on her horse, and, urging Grani to flight, sped away through the clouds.

Wotan, left alone with the Robber, turned towards him in contemptuous anger. Before his gaze Hunding sank to the earth in death.

Suddenly the King God burst into supreme wrath.

" Brünnhilde, who has disobeyed me, must be punished!" he cried. And, leaping upon his war-horse, he was gone through the clouds.

Motif of Siegmund and Sieglinde's Love

Motif of the Walküres' Ride

Motif of Brünnhilde's Pleading

Slumber Motif

## CHAPTER III

### BRÜNNHILDE'S PUNISHMENT

IT was a custom of the Walküres to meet every evening after their wild rides, at a rock called "The Walküres' Stone," and thence go on to Walhalla.

Upon the afternoon of the combat which had proved fatal to the Volsung, the Walküres arrived one after the other at the rock. Only one was missing—Wotan's favorite, Brünnhilde.

The maidens sang merrily their Hoyotoho, waved their spears and climbed the rocks, and kept a sharp lookout for Grani's appearance in the clouds. But it was very late before Brünnhilde was anywhere to be seen. When she came, she brought with her Sieglinde, whom she was supporting. In answer to her sisters' anxious inquiries, the Walküre told them of her disobedience and Sieglinde's sorrow, and begged them to protect Siegmund's wife, and herself as well.

"And see, O sisters, if Wotan draws nigh!" she begged.

"A thunder-cloud approaches," called Ortlinda, one of the Walküres, from her high pinnacle of rock.

"The clouds grow thicker," cried Waltrauta. "Our father comes," they exclaimed in unison.

"Shelter this woman," begged Brünnhilde. For she knew that Wotan, in his rage, might kill the wife of the warrior whom he had overthrown. But the maidens feared their father's anger, and would give no aid. So, at last, Brünnhilde told Sieglinde to fly and hide herself in the forest, and that she, the Walküre, would remain behind to bear the brunt of Wotan's anger. Brünnhilde drew from under her shield the splinters of Nothung, which she had picked up on the battle-field, and gave them with words of kindness and comfort to Sieglinde, who, murmuring tender thanks, sped away into the woods and was gone.

Then even Brünnhilde's brave heart began to fail her. A great storm had arisen, and amid the crash of thunder came Wotan's voice calling her name in tones of anger. Trembling, she took her place in the centre of the group of maidens, concealed from view by them.

Surrounded by red light came Wotan, having left his war-steed snorting in the wood.

"Where is Brünnhilde?" he demanded. But the Walküres, in trembling tones, merely asked the cause of his anger. In growing rage, Wotan commanded Brünnhilde to come forward and receive her punishment, reproaching her in scornful words for hiding among her sisters.

Quietly the Walküre came out from among them, and stood before him. She was quite ready to receive her sentence, whatever it might be, and bent her head to listen to her father's words.

Her punishment, Wotan told her, was to be this: She was to be laid in helpless sleep, at the

mercy of the first passer-by who might choose
to awaken her. Him she must follow as his
wife, for, when she was awakened from her
sleep, she would be a woman—a goddess no
longer.

Heart-broken, Brünnhilde sank to the ground
with a cry. To be made mortal seemed to her
the most terrible punishment possible. And it
seemed so to the other Walküres as well. They
besought the King God to have mercy on their
sister, but he was firm.

Amid wails of despair and pity for Brünnhilde,
the Walküres separated and rushed wildly out of
sight in all directions. Only the echoes of their
cries and the last faint sound of their horses'
hoofs remained as they rode off through the
clouds.

The storm died away. All was quiet now.
Slowly Brünnhilde rose from where she lay and
pleadingly spoke to her father, asking pardon for
her disobedience and begging for some mercy
and tenderness. At last, when she found that,
though he still loved her as dearly as ever, he
was firm in his decision, she asked only one fa-
vor of him—a last one—that he should place a
circle of flame about the rock where she was to
be laid asleep, flame so fierce and high that only

a brave man might come through it and awaken her.

Wotan consented, and, overcome by his love for her, drew her into his arms in a last, sad embrace. He bade her farewell with a tenderness that comforted her even then, and, stooping, kissed her long and lovingly.

Her eyes closed. Her head sank back against his shoulder. Laying her on a rock that made a rude couch, he placed her shield on her arm and her spear at her side. He looked down with deepest sorrow on the face of this, his most beautiful child, the War Goddess, and then, raising his spear, commanded Logi to light a ring of fire about the rock.

Great billows of flame spread from left to right, and glowed in a brilliant circle about the sleeping goddess, casting a dim glare on her figure, and lighting up the quiet night-sky.

Standing in the red firelight, Wotan once more stretched out his spear in a spell, and pronounced these words:

"Only he who fears not my spear can pass through this fiery bar."

And, so saying, he passed from out the charmed circle and left behind him the Walküre in her long, fire-watched sleep, to be broken only by

one who feared not even the spear of Wotan,
the king of the gods.

The Sleep of the Walküre

# Part III

# SIEGFRIED

Motif of Mime's Meditation

# PRELUDE

WHEN Sieglinde ran into the woods with the pieces of the broken sword, Nothung, she took shelter in a cave where a wicked old dwarf lived alone. There a little boy was born. But Sieglinde had never thoroughly recovered from the shock of her husband's death. The way through the woods had been difficult, and she had endured great hardships; so one day she called the Dwarf to her and gave him the broken sword, telling him to keep it for her son until he grew old enough to have a weapon of his own, and she told the Dwarf that she was Sieglinde, and that her husband had been Siegmund, the Volsung, and she finally said that she wanted the child to be named Siegfried; then she sank back and died. And so Siegfried, who was a very little baby then, never, really, saw either his father or mother.

The only father he knew, as he grew older,

was the Dwarf, who was none other than Mime Alberich's half-brother. And he could not help knowing that Mime was wicked and sly, though the Dwarf pretended to love his foster-son, and tried to arouse some love in return.

Now, perhaps, you wonder, if Mime was so wicked, why he took care of the boy. I will tell you.

Mime, like every one else, wanted the Rhine-gold, and could not get it, for Fafner, the Drag-on, guarded it by night and day at Hate Hole. And being as sly and evil-minded as the rest of the Nibelungs, he had concocted a plot by which he thought he could obtain it. He hoped Sieg-fried, when he grew older, would slay Fafner with the sword Nothung, and win the Rhine-gold. You see he hoped to accomplish Fafner's death through Siegfried, just as Wotan had once tried to do through Siegmund. Only, af-ter Siegfried had attained the Gold, Mime hoped to be able to poison him and steal from him the treasure.

But, to accomplish this, the broken sword must be mended, and this Mime could not do. Its splintered edges baffled even him — clever smith as he was. So he set to work forging other swords, and trying to fashion a blade keen

enough to satisfy the boy-Volsung, and also to
kill the Dragon at Hate Hole. But every weapon he made Siegfried broke into pieces, and demanded a stronger and still stronger sword, until
Mime was in despair.

It angered him terribly, too, that Siegfried,
more by instinct than anything else, knew how
wicked his heart was, and how full of bad, cruel
thoughts. The little, dark Nibelung could not
understand how the boy, beautiful as the sun,
golden-haired and keen-eyed, strong of limb and
true of heart, loved to roam in the wide for-
ests all the day, merrily blowing his silver horn
and making friends with the woodland creatures,
only returning to Mime's cave at night. He
could not realize the pleasure that the soft forest voices gave to the youth just growing into
manhood; how he loved the wolves and bears
better than the cringing, evil-eyed, horrible little
Dwarf in the cave at home—the only home he
knew.

As for Siegfried, the only thing he wondered
at was that he ever went back to the cave at all.
Why did he not roam away forever into the
forest, search out that far, strange place called
the world, that really seemed as if it must be a
different universe from the one in which he lived?

5

He could not tell.   He only knew that a strange, irresistible something seemed to draw him back to Mime's side every night—a something he could not explain or even understand.   Meanwhile time passed.

Motif of Forest Life, sometimes called Motif of Love Life

Motif of the Forging of Nothung

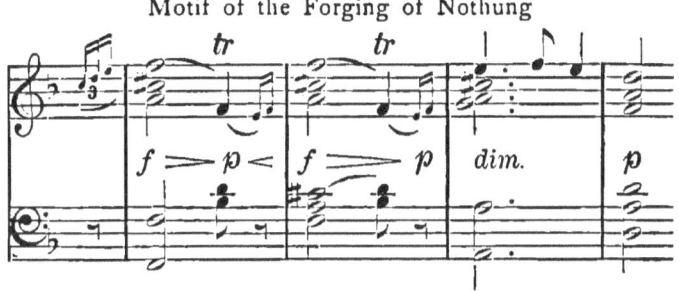

"No-thung! No-thung! No-ta-ble Sword!"

## CHAPTER I

### SIEGFRIED AND MIME

THE cave was a dark one, but it was not altogether a bad place in which to live. It was as lofty as a stately cathedral, and the Dwarf's forge, built on one side, lent a fitful red light and a little warmth to the dim, cold atmosphere.

Skins of animals gave it a semblance of comfort ; and, indeed, to a wild creature like Siegfried, it would have been a most desirable home had it not been for the continual presence of Mime.  On the day on which I will open my story, Mime was sitting on a low stool trying to fashion a sword which would not break in the hands of the impetuous young Volsung, who, at that particular moment, was, as usual, out in the woods with his friends, the wild beasts.  As he hammered, Mime grumbled crossly because he had to work forever with swords that seemed of no use to the crazy boy, who insisted on smashing them all, and racing off to the woods, merely demanding as he went a better and a stronger weapon.

"There is a blade that he could not break," muttered the Nibelung, as he worked.  "Nothung he would find firm in his hands, but I cannot weld the splinters.  Ah! if I could, I should be well repaid."  He paused, and then went on, mysteriously murmuring to himself :

"Fafner, the great, wicked worm ! Well guards he the Rhinegold.  Only Siegfried can overthrow him.  This can only be done by Nothung, I feel sure.  And, alas! I cannot shape Nothung, the sword."

He began to hammer once more, grumbling continually because Siegfried insisted that he should make swords, and snarling with rage because every weapon he forged fell to pieces in the boy's strong hands.

Suddenly, from without, came a clear, merry voice, shouting a blithe "Hoyho!" and the next moment in came Siegfried himself, leading a great bear, which he had harnessed with a bit of rope.

"Ask the foolish smith if he has finished the sword, Bruin!" he cried to the bear, and, holding back the great creature firmly, he pretended to chase Mime, who, springing behind the anvil, cried, savagely:

"Take him away! I don't want the bear! I have done my best with your sword."

"Good!" laughed the boy. "Good-bye, Bruin: run away," and he freed the great creature, sending him lumbering off into the woods again.

Then, turning to the trembling Nibelung, he again asked for the sword, and Mime handed it to him. The young Volsung took it into his hands quickly, scorn on his handsome face and anger in his eyes. He was dressed in a wild forest costume of wolf-skins, and his yellow hair curled over his shoulders. He, indeed, made a

great contrast to Mime, and one could not wonder that they did not get on well together.

"What a toy!" he cried out. "Do you call
this a sword?" and, striking it on the anvil, he
broke the blade into a hundred slivers, and then
burst into a rage with the smith, who had pretended to give him a sword fit for battle, and
had shaped him so foolish a switch, as he called
it. And finally, thoroughly out of breath, he
flung himself upon the stone couch at one side,
and not all Mime's coaxings could appease his
anger. He finally confessed that he did not
know why he ever returned to the cave, because, he said frankly, he could not help detest-
ing the Dwarf, and was much happier when away
from him. And then he broke into a passionate
description of the wood-life he loved so well; the
mating of the birds in the spring-time, and the
way they loved and helped each other; the care
that the mother deer lavished upon her little
ones; the tenderness among all the forest creatures that seemed so beautiful and mysterious
to him.

"I learned watching them," said Siegfried, almost sorrowfully, "what love must be. Mime,
where is she whom *I* may call mother?"

"Nonsense!" said Mime, and tried to draw

Siegfried's mind away from the dangerous topic;
for he had never told him anything about his
parents, always calling him his own son.  And
he feared the boy's anger if he should ever know
that he had been deceived.

But, thoroughly aroused, the young Volsung
fiercely demanded the names of his father and
mother, declaring that he was far too unlike
Mime to be his son.  At last the Nibelung confessed the truth, and told him the story of his
mother's death, and of how she had left her child
in his care.  And, when the boy asked for proof,
he slowly crept away, to return with the broken
sword Nothung, the mending of which was so
hard a riddle even to his sly brain.

Wildly excited, Siegfried commanded him to
work at it anew and do his best to weld the
pieces; and, with a shout of delight and hope,
he went merrily away into the woods, leaving
Mime in saddest, deepest perplexity.

Despairing, he murmured at the hopelessness
of the task, which his rather unruly young charge
had set him, and was sitting, a picture of dis-
couragement and misery, when from the dark
woods came a stranger clad as a wanderer, and
bearing a great spear.  He advanced to the door
of the cave and asked in slow, grave tones for

rest and shelter. Mime was at first frightened, then angry, and finally refused to harbor the strange guest, until the Wanderer made the following proposal: Mime was to ask him three questions, and if they were not correctly answered the host should have the privilege of cutting off his guest's head. To this Mime consented, and, after a little thought, thus chose his first question:

"Tell me what is the race down in the earth's depths?"

And the Wanderer made answer: "In the earth's depths dwell the Nibelungs. Nibelheim is their land. Once they were ruled by Black Alberich, who owned a magic Ring by which he possessed untold wealth. What is the next question?"

Again Mime pondered.

"Now, Wanderer, since you know so much of the earth's depths," he said, "tell me what is the race that dwells upon its surface?"

"The giants dwell upon its surface. Two of them, Fasolt and Fafner, fought for Black Alberich's hoard. Fafner guards it now as a dragon. Put your third question!"

"What race dwells in the sky above?" demanded Mime.

And the Wanderer answered, majestically:

"The gods dwell above in Walhalla. Their King is Wotan, who owns a spear made of the World-Ash. With that spear he rules the world."

And, as he spoke, Wotan, the Wanderer, struck the earth with the haft he held, and a peal of thunder crashed suddenly out upon the silence.

As Mime cowered, terror-stricken, recognizing his guest, the Wanderer again spoke.

He said it was only fair that he should have the same right he had given to Mime, and declared that he should ask three questions with the privilege of cutting off the Nibelung's head if they were not answered aright.

"Tell me, O Dwarf," he began, "what was that race which Wotan loved, and yet treated harshly?"

"The Volsungs," answered Mime, partially recovering from his terror. "Siegmund and Sieglinde were descended from the race. Siegfried is their son — the strongest Volsung who ever lived."

"Well answered!" said the Wanderer. "Now listen and reply! A sly Nibelung watches Siegfried, knowing that he is fated to kill Fafner, the Dragon. What sword must he use to kill him?"

" Nothung!" cried Mime, eagerly. "Nothung is the name of the sword. Siegmund once drew it from a great tree. It was broken by the spear of Wotan. Now a clever smith "—and he rubbed his hands gleefully—"understands all this, and he hoards well the splinters, knowing that with these alone can Siegfried kill the Dragon."

The Wanderer burst out into laughter.

" But who will mend the sword?" he asked.

Mime sprang to his feet in despair, filled with terror and rage; for that was the one question he could not answer—that was his riddle, his everlasting mystery.

Quietly Wotan rose from the hearth where he had been sitting.

" I gave you three chances to ask me the question which I have now asked you. Foolishly, you let them all slip by. Listen while I answer it! *Only he who has never felt fear can forge Nothung anew.*"

He strode to the door of the cave, and there paused, looking back.

" Guard well your head, O Dwarf! I leave it to him who knows not fear."

Smiling quietly, the Wanderer disappeared in the wood's depths, and thunder and lightning followed him as he went.

Mime was left — puzzled, despairing, terror-stricken. His vivid imagination began to conjure up before him visions of Fafner, the Dragon, and he had fallen behind the anvil, so great was his fear, when Siegfried came hastily in, asking once more for the sword.

Mime, creeping out from behind the anvil, could not at once collect his scattered wits, and merely muttered :

"*Only he who has never felt fear can forge Nothung anew.* My wits are too wise for that job."

Finally, as Siegfried demanded why he had not worked at the sword, he said, slowly :

" I was fearing for your sake."

"*Fearing!*" said Siegfried. " What do you mean by fearing?"

Mime described the tremblings, shudderings, and quakings aroused by fear, and Siegfried remarked, as he finished :

"All that must seem very queer. I rather think I should like to feel all that — but how shall I learn ?"

Mime, delighted, told him of Fafner, and said that the Dragon would teach him, or any one else, the art of fearing, and ended by promising to lead him to Hate Hole the next day.

" Does the world lie that way?" asked the boy.

" To Hate Hole it is close at hand," responded the wicked little Nibelung, beginning to feel rapture glow in his heart.

But, when Siegfried again demanded the sword, the smith fell once more into despair, wailing that he could not shape it, that only one who knew not fear could forge it anew.

Straight to the hearth sprang the strong young Volsung with the splinters of Nothung.

" My father's blade will I forge!" he cried; and he began to move about merrily, brightening the fire and hunting for the file with which to work on the broken blade.

Mime watched him with wondering eyes. So swiftly and well did he work that even the clever smith could not understand. And, as he dragged at the rope of the bellows and blew up the fire in the forge, this is the song that Siegfried sang:

> " Nothung, Nothung, notable sword!
>   Who did thy bright steel shiver?
> To shreds I have shattered the noble blade,
>   In the pot I shall melt each sliver.

> " Oho, oho, aha, aha, oho!
>   Bellows blow,
>   Brighten the glow!

SIEGFRIED AT THE FORGE

"Far in the woodlands wild and fair,
'Mid the thickets, a tree felled I;
I have burned the brown ash into coal,
On the hearth I have piled it high.

"Oho, oho, aha, aha, oho!
Bellows blow,
Brighten the glow!

"The coal from the tree how bravely it flames!
The fire how fierce to see!
It sends its wild sparks scattering far,
And the steel shreds it smelts for me.

"Oho, oho, aha, aha, oho!
Bellows blow,
Brighten the glow!"

Meanwhile Mime was busy about something, too. He was preparing a poison for Siegfried, which he did not intend to give him until after he had slain the Dragon. Round, round the cave capered the Dwarf, filled with delight at the pleasant prospect he saw before him.

At last the sword was finished, and Siegfried fitted it into its handle. It was mended anew.

Waving it aloft, he broke into a new verse of his song:

"Nothung, Nothung, new and young!
I have given thee life and might!
Dead and desolate hast thou lain,
Now leapest thou fearless and bright.

Show now thy sheen to the cowards all,
Shatter deceit, and on falsehood fall."

He sprang to the anvil and swung the blade high in the air.

"See, Mime, so serves Siegfried's sword!" he shouted, exultantly.

Down came the flashing steel, and the anvil was shattered in pieces. Mime sank to the ground in terror, but, holding his father's sword above his head, and filled with absolute joy and triumph, stood young Siegfried — he who had never felt fear, and who had forged Nothung anew.

Siegfried Motif

Motif of the Niebelungs' Hate

Siegfried's Horn-call

## CHAPTER II

### HATE HOLE

TO Hate Hole, in the dark time before dawn, came the Wanderer, and found Alberich waiting and watching near the entrance. The Dwarf was fearfully enraged at the sight of the old god, whom he hated with all the strength of his wicked Nibelung soul. He burst into a torrent of abuse and anger as Wotan drew near, speaking of the broken promise of the giants and the deceit by which the Gold had been obtained from the Nibelungs, and again threatening the downfall of the gods when the Ring should come back to his hands. The Wanderer answered quietly that a hero was even then drawing near through the woods—a hero fated to kill Fafner and obtain the Gold; and, with hidden sarcasm, he bade the Dwarf attempt to use the youth for his own ends.

The King God believed in the workings of Fate. The Norns wove continually, and all that they wove came to pass. No one could change the histories wound into their golden cord, until the Dusk of the Gods had come, when they also would, in the Last Twilight, be gone forever. So, feeling as he did, it mattered very little whom he aided, whom he harmed. He even went so far as to arouse Fafner for Alberich, and ask him to give the Dwarf the Ring. The old Dragon snarled and yawned and went to sleep again. The Wanderer turned to the Nibelung, with a great laugh.

"Listen!" he said. "Remember, O Alberich, what I say. All things work in nature's course. You can alter nothing."

And, so saying, he vanished in the dark woods, and a faint, pale flicker of lightning shot through the forest as he went. Alberich crept hastily into a crevice in the rocks on one side, and the dawn broke just as two figures came into the little green glade by Hate Hole.

The figures were those of Siegfried and Mime;
for the Nibelung, true to his word, had led
the boy to the place where he was to learn to
fear.

" If you do not hastily discover fear here, my
dear boy, you never will anywhere," said the
Dwarf, with a chuckle. And he described at
great length the means which Fafner would use
to teach the art, saying that the Dragon's breath
was fire, and his twisting tail strong enough to
crush any hero. But Siegfried merely laughed,
and said that he would find the great worm's
heart and strike Nothung into that; and then he
bade Mime be gone. The Nibelung crept away
out of sight among the trees, and as he went he
muttered, in an exasperated undertone :

" Fafner and Siegfried ! Siegfried and Fafner ! Oh, that each might kill the other !"

The boy, left alone, sat under a linden-tree,
looking up through the branches. At first Mime's
figure pervaded his brain, and he could not help
remembering the horrible little creature. But,
after a while, thoughts of his mother crept in —
very vague and formless thoughts — for this forest youth had never in his life seen a woman.
Leaning back, he gave himself up to the en-
chantment of the summer-day, dreaming boyish

6

dreams, and listening to the forest voices all around him.

Have you ever sat in a great, green wood and watched the soft flickering shadows from the little leaves overhead dance back and forth on the moss? Have you heard the great surge of music made of a thousand tiny sounds, the hum of little, unseen insects, the ripple of far-away brooks, the faint sigh of the wind in the tall reeds, the rustling of the trees, the melodies that seemed made by the touch of some master-hand on a great harp? That was what Siegfried saw and heard that summer day when he lay under the linden-tree and dreamed day-dreams.

After a while a little bird began to sing in the tree above him, and after listening for a moment, and wondering whether it brought him a message from his mother, he resolved to try to imitate it, remembering that Mime had once said that some people were able to talk with the birds. So he fashioned a flute out of a reed and tried to play upon it the melody that the bird sang. Finally, however, he gave it up in despair, and instead, as he began to feel lonely, he blew a loud blast on his horn—to bring him a friend, he said to himself.

THE DEATH OF THE DRAGON

And what sort of a friend do you think it brought him?

Well, it waked Fafner, the monster worm; and he dragged his huge scaly body to the door of the cave and peered out, and you may fancy like what sort of a friend he looked.

Siegfried burst out into laughter when he saw him.

"At last!" he cried, merrily. "My call has brought me something truly lovely!"

"What is that?" growled Fafner, glaring at him as though he were a small insect of some sort.

"Hey! You can talk, can you?" cried Siegfried. "Being so wise, you should be able to teach me how to fear. I have come for that."

Fafner laughed, and showed his teeth, bidding the boy come and be eaten.

"I come, growler!" said the young Volsung; and, drawing his sword, he sprang boldly at the great, hideous creature at the cave's opening. Fafner reared to receive him, and the combat began. It was fierce, but not very long, for the boy was strong and Nothung was sharp, and soon Alberich's spell had again worked its misery; and, indeed, it could be said of the dying Dragon that his death was sad—his life had been a failure.

Before he died he told Siegfried to beware of Mime, and then spoke slowly and sadly of the race of giants that had come to an end.

"Siegfried," he began once more — but he never finished, poor old Dragon; for, just at the word, he rolled over and died. And that was the end of the race of giants.

Stooping down, the young warrior drew his sword from out the Dragon's heart. In so doing, a drop of blood fell on his hand. It burned like the cruellest fire. He raised it quickly to his mouth to relieve the smarting; and, as the blood touched his lips, a strange thing happened — he could understand the language of birds. Yes, as the same little singer that he had heard before began to twitter, he could understand what it was saying to him.

"Hey! Siegfried will have now the Nibelung's hoard! He will find the hoard in the hole. The Tarnhelm would aid him through wonderful deeds; but the Ring would give him might over the world."

With a laugh and a word of thanks to the little singer, the boy stepped into the cave to look for the treasure. At the same minute Mime crept near from behind the clump of bushes. Alberich sprang out from his rocky crevice, and the two little Nibelungs met, snarling, capering, and making faces with rage.

Each claimed the Ring, and called the other names, and each proved himself a marvel in wickedness and greed, and they were nearing a point when blows were not far off when the hero himself stepped out from the cave with the Tarnhelm thrust into his belt, and the Rhinegold Ring upon his finger. The dwarfs hastened out of sight.

The heaped-up hoard of the Nibelungs, Siegfried had left, for he knew little of its use, and he cared nothing for wealth. Indeed, both Helm and Ring he had taken only because the bird had so advised him. He could not fancy what good either of them would do him.

" Hey ! Siegfried has now the Helm and the Ring !" sang the wood-bird in the tree. " Trust not in Mime ! The Dragon's blood will tell Siegfried what the treacherous Dwarf really means."

At this point, Mime himself appeared, smiling and bowing, and holding in his hands a horn of wine for Siegfried. He said that it would refresh the boy after his labors, but we know that it was poisoned. Thanks to the Dragon's blood, Siegfried knew it too, and read all the cruel thoughts that were passing through Mime's

brain, and, in a burst of anger, he finally raised
his sword and killed the treacherous Dwarf with
one blow.

So that was the end of the Nibelung Mime,
the cleverest smith, they say, that ever lived in
the world—even though he could not fashion
Nothung, the sword.   From a black crevice in
the rocks came Alberich's laugh, loud and mocking—the echo of his own wicked thoughts.

Siegfried turned away wearily, and, seating himself under the linden, listened for the bird's song
again.   As it did not come at once, he looked up
into the branches and spoke:

" You  seem  very  happy,  flying  among  your
brothers and sisters, birdie.   But I am all alone.
I have no brothers nor sisters, and my father and
mother are both dead.   Tell me where I may find
a loving friend.   I have called one so often, but
none ever comes."   He sighed.   " Sing now, sing,"
he begged ; and again the bird's twitter sounded
from among the leaves above him.

" Hey!   Siegfried  has  slain  now  the  wicked
Dwarf.   I know where he'll find a glorious bride.
On  a rock she sleeps amid fire.   If he passed
through  the  blaze  and  awakened  her,  Brünnhilde would then be his."

Wild with excitement and joy, Siegfried sprang

to his feet and asked if he would really be able to do this.

" Brünnhilde is won only by him who knows not fear," said the wood-bird, and flew off before him, guiding him through the woods.

In a transport of joy Siegfried followed, and, shouting with delight, he began his journey to the far-away rock in its circle of flame, where the Walküre, in her long penance of sleep, waited for the hero brave enough to pass through the fire and awaken her.

**Song of the Wood-Bird**

" Hey ! Siegfried has slain now the wicked dwarf!

I know where he'll find a glo-ri-ous bride."

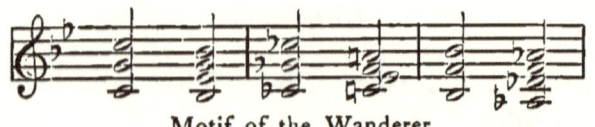

Motif of the Wanderer

Erda Motif

## CHAPTER III

### THE MOUNTAIN PASS

A WILD storm was raging among the mountains. Great winds swept down from the high peaks and up from the valleys and crashed roaring through the woods. The thunder rumbled, and flashes of blue lightning shot across the dark sky. The heart of the tempest seemed to be at a rocky pass just below the path that led up to the Walküres' rock.

Here, before a huge black cleft in the side of the mountain, stood the Wanderer, the wild storm all about him. With outstretched spear he was singing a strange chant, an awakening song, down into the black chasm before him; singing it to the wise woman of the world, Erda, the Earth Witch.

He called her by name, and bade her rise from her sleep and speak with him; and, as he chanted, a faint blue light glowed in the chasm, and Erda rose slowly from the black depths. Frost seemed to cling to her garments, and light gleamed all about her. Her face wore the same look of mystery as when she came so many years before to warn Wotan against the Ring.

In slow, dreamy tones she asked what the Wanderer wished, and why he had aroused her from her slumber of wisdom. He answered that he had come to ask her to prophesy once more; to tell him the wonders that she had dreamed.

"I sleep and dream!" answered the Earth Goddess. "I dream and search for wisdom. But, while I sleep, the Norns are awake. They weave their rope and spin. Why do you not seek them and ask them your questions?"

The Wanderer answered that they could only weave the histories of the world, but that she, in her wisdom, could, perhaps, tell him how to avert coming ill. But Erda shook her head dreamily, as though in a trance, and answered that she could tell him nothing; that the ways of the world bewildered her, and that she longed to return into her dark chasm and dream once more.

But Wotan restrained her. He told her of the Walküre's disobedience and his own wrath. He spoke of the sorrow and grief that weighed heavily on his mind, of his forebodings, and that the Dusk of the Gods seemed nearer and nearer. And, after asking again for counsel, in vain, he said that he had grown to feel very little dread of the Dusk of the Gods. It was destiny, and he almost longed for it. And he spoke tenderly of the Volsung, who was even then drawing near to pass through the flame and free the Walküre from her chains of sleep.

When she was awakened, Wotan said—gifted with the power of prophecy for a moment—she would, by some deed, release the world from the sadness that it had labored under for so long, and she would expiate the old sin of the stealing of the Gold that was the beginning of the end of the Golden Age.

" Then sleep once more !" said the Wanderer. " Dream and foresee the end ! Away, Erda—all-fearing, all-sorrowing ; away to eternal sleep !"

Slowly the Goddess of the Earth slipped down into the darkness, and the blue light faded away.

The storm had ceased. Only faint, distant rumbles of thunder sounded in the high hills; faint, shivering winds crept through the moaning forest-trees, and a little light stole over the mountain pass from the rising moon.

From the depths of the forest came Siegfried, staring about him and looking in vain for his small feathered guide.

It had vanished, and he concluded, after a moment, that he had better go on alone, find his way to the fire-circle without a guide, and awaken the sleeping maiden. He started up the pass; but, suddenly, a voice said slowly close beside him:

" Where are you going, boy?"

He turned and saw the Wanderer.

" Perhaps he can tell me the way," thought Siegfried; and, aloud, he answered: " I am seeking for a rock surrounded by fire. A woman sleeps there whom I will wake."

The Wanderer asked him who suggested such an idea to him, and questioned him closely as to his life and deeds.

Siegfried answered simply and frankly, until,

when he spoke of his good sword, the Wanderer burst into a loud peal of laughter.

"Why do you laugh at me?" asked the boy. "Listen, old questioner! Tell me the way, or, if you cannot do that, say nothing at all," for he was in a thoroughly bad humor, and in the woods he had never been taught to accord old age much honor. So he strode up to the Wanderer and demanded that he should tell him the way, threatening to serve him like Mime if he insisted on barring the pass. For Wotan was standing directly before the rocky way, and, as Siegfried was in great haste, it exasperated him.

"You will not tell me, then?" he said, finally. "Then get out of my way! I will find the rock for myself. My little bird-friend showed me in which direction the slumbering woman lies."

"The bird!" said Wotan, wrathfully. "It fled to save its life. The King-Ravens barred its way."

For the god had sent his two great birds to turn back the little guide, just as he himself intended to attempt to turn back Siegfried.

He had said in his spell, when he left Brünnhilde sleeping on the rock: "Only one who fears not my spear can pass through the fire bar." Now, this must be the test. Would this strong, beautiful boy recoil before the haft made of the World-Ash, or would the Dusk of the Gods come through human courage, overthrowing the might of the gods?

The Wanderer stretched out his great spear, the spear which had strange figures upon it representing Law and Knowledge; the spear which was typical of the wisdom and the power of the gods; the spear upon which Nothung, the sword, had once been shattered.

"The weapon you swing," said the Wanderer, "was once shivered upon this haft. It will again snap on the Eternal Spear."

Siegfried drew his sword.

"Then you are my father's enemy!" he cried. "Then you broke his defence! Stretch out your spear! My sword shall break it in pieces!"

And a great peal of thunder crashed among the hills as Nothung broke the Eternal Spear with which Wotan had ruled the world.

The old god stooped and gathered up the broken pieces of his once mighty haft, and, with slow steps, passed out of sight in the forest depths. The Dusk of the Gods seemed, indeed, at hand.

As Siegfried stood gazing after his retreating figure, he suddenly became conscious of a great glare that seemed to grow brighter and brighter every moment. Looking up the pass before him, he beheld great billows of flame rolling about a high peak — billows that seemed to surge down towards him as though defying him to conquer them.

"Ha! Wonderful glow!" shouted Siegfried. "In fire will I bathe! In fire will I find my bride!"

And blowing a long, clear call on his silver horn, he sprang into the sea of flame, and passed up the steep, fiery way that led to the Walküres' rock.

Love Motif

Motif of Siegfried the Protector

## CHAPTER IV

### THE WALKÜRES' ROCK

THE fire rolled and surged about him, the great red flames twisted around him, and in many colors the vistas opened here and there like rainbow avenues. For the colors in fire are more beautiful than those in an opal.

As he passed up the steep way, and trampled the flames and beat them back, laughing at their scorching heat, they began to burn lower and sank into a narrow, bright circle of fire behind him; unobtrusive and not at all fierce, just, in fact, what they had been until a hero drew near to pass through them. Then they had done their best to keep him from their fair, sleeping captive; but they were conquered, the wild, bright flames; and they died down to almost nothing as the Volsung, still blowing a merry call on his horn, sprang up the rocks to the summit of the mountain.

It was quiet and calm there, full of deep peace and silence. It seemed as if even the trees and flowers were asleep. No sound broke the stillness, no leaf moved or insect darted. It was as though Nature were laying her finger on her lip and saying, "Hush — hush! This place is enchanted."

It was broad day, and the blue sky, reaching overhead, seemed to smile down on the young hero as he stood gazing wonderingly about him.

On one side stretched the dark wood, reaching down the mountain-side — the wood into which his mother had run, bearing the splinters of Nothung, so many years before. As he looked into the dark depths he was amazed to see a war-horse asleep under the trees. It was Grani, who had fallen under the same spell as his mistress. As Siegfried took a step forward, he suddenly stopped short in overpowering surprise. For before him, upon a rock, lay a figure clad in brightest steel, with shield and spear and helmet gleaming in the sun.

"Is it a warrior?" thought the young Volsung, drawing near—for Mime had described to him the bright armor the great heroes wore in battle. "Perhaps," thought Siegfried, as he bent over the sleeper, "he would rest better if his helmet were loosened." And he unfastened it carefully and took it off. Masses of golden curling hair gleamed like sunny clouds about the fair face of the Walküre.

"Ah, how beautiful!" cried Siegfried, softly. "The face is like that of the sun smiling between mists."

He bent down still lower.

"How heavily he breathes! I would better open his armor," said the boy. Drawing his sword, he cut off the mail in which the sleeper was arrayed. When the last ring was loosened and he had lifted off the suit of mail-armor, he started erect, filled with a strange, wonderful feeling that he had never known before. The sleeping Walküre, no longer dressed in steel like a warrior, but in long, white, womanly robes, was so marvellous and beautiful that this lionhearted young Volsung felt fear at last in

7

the presence of the first woman he had ever seen.

Timidly he drew near, wondering how he should arouse her.

"Awaken, beautiful woman!" he cried, tremulously. But she did not hear. At last he bent over her and kissed her.

Brünnhilde opened her eyes.

Starting up, she lifted both arms towards the sky, and cried, in glad though solemn tones,

"Hail, O sun! Hail, O light! Hail, O glorious day! Long was my sleep—I am awakened! Where is the hero who awakes me?"

The young Volsung, drawing timidly near, answered that it was he who had come through the fire and awakened her, and that his name was Siegfried; and he said, too, that, as she had first aroused fear in his heart, she must bring his courage back to him. Passionately, he told her that he loved her; but Brünnhilde could not remember that she was no longer a Walküre, and at first she did not want to be a woman and a mortal's wife—however great that mortal might be.

But, after a time, with a sudden great rush of passion, she felt in some strange way that she cared no longer for the gods and their glory, and loved only Siegfried, and longed to serve him and be his wife. So she promised to marry him, and she said that the Norns might break their rope of histories, for the Dusk of the Gods drew near.

She taught Siegfried many strange things and much wisdom—the wisdom of the gods. And she gave him her weapons, forgot that she had ever been a Walküre, and loved him with all her heart.

Motif of Peace

# Part IV

# THE DUSK OF THE GODS, OR
# *GÖTTERDÄMMERUNG*

Motif of the World-Ash-Tree

# PRELUDE

HOLDING in his hand his broken spear, the king of the gods wended his way to Walhalla. He sent forth stanch messengers to hew the World - Ash into a thousand pieces and pile them high about the gods' palace. Then he assembled round him his heroes and the Walküres and the rest of the divinities, and sat in silence awaiting the Dusk of the Gods.

All the gods, far and wide, knew that the Last Twilight was impending ; and fate relentlessly led all things to the end. To the Walküres' rock came the Norns in the gray of dawn to spin. From hand to hand passed the golden cord. Each told a history in gloomy, chanting measures.

The oldest Norn sang of the days when the World-Ash was green and the Fountain of Wisdom purled softly in the shadow of the wide branches. She sang of Wotan's coming to the spring and drinking; of the tearing of the limb from the World-Ash; of the withering of the great tree. Her song ceased. She flung the cord to her sister.

The second Norn wound slowly as she sang. Her tale was of the making of the great spear with which Wotan had ruled the world until one stronger than the gods had shivered the haft and overpowered the Ruler. She sang of how Wotan had now ordered that the World-Ash should be broken and piled about Walhalla. She paused, and the youngest Norn took the rope.

She sang of the bright palace where Wotan sat among the gods and heroes, with the great fagots from the World-Ash heaped around him. She sang that, when these fagots should be lighted and Walhalla burned, the Dusk of the Gods would come.

They sang of many strange events — these Norns — events of the past, of the present, of the future. They sang of the circle of fire lit by Logi about the rock. They sang of the Rhinegold stolen by Alberich; they sang long and sadly of the gods and their king.

"The web is tangled," said the first Norn.

"Alberich's spell tears at the strands," said the second, and flung it to the third.

BRÜNNHILDE ON THE WALKÜRES' ROCK

"I cannot reach the rope — it is too short," said the youngest, putting out her hand.

The cord snapped. It had stretched across the past, but it could not touch the future. It was, indeed, too short.

"It breaks!" wailed the Norns, crouching in dread, as the faint light of day appeared.

"At an end is our wisdom!" they murmured in chorus, and wound the broken bits of the rope about their gray-shrouded bodies; then fled like mist into the earth, down to their mother, Erda, the all-wise one, she who had first prophesied the Dusk of the Gods.

\*  \*  \*  \*  \*  \*

When she had taught him all the wisdom that she knew, and given him all she had, Brünnhilde bade her hero go forth into the world and win fame and honor by great deeds. He must journey to the far lands peopled by brave men and high heroes and prove his courage and his strength. She would wait for him patiently, and he would come back to her when he had made all men know and honor him.

She gave him Grani, her stanch war-horse, and he placed on her finger as a parting love-gift the beautiful bright Ring that he had won at Hate Hole, and then he bade her farewell, and blithely passed down the mountain - side, blowing a clear, merry blast on his horn.

Brünnhilde stood on the Walküres' rock and gazed yearningly after him, and the young hero went forth into far lands to know men and do great deeds, and find at last that strange place called the world.

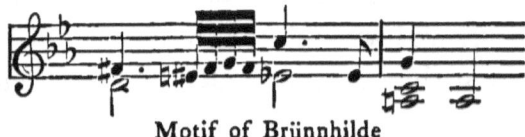

Motif of Brünnhilde

Motif of the Gibichungs

*poco f*

Motif of Hagen

## CHAPTER I

### THE HALL OF THE GIBICHUNGS

ON the banks of the river Rhine there lived a great warrior named Gunther, who was one of a valiant race called Gibichungs. He was the head of a great tribe of kinsmen and vassals, and his lands were wide and his halls spacious. His sister, Gutrune, was a maiden very fair and sweet to look upon, as beautiful as her brother was brave. They were both generous and noble, and would have done nothing but good all their lives had it not been for the evil influence of their wicked half-brother Hagen, the son of Alberich, the Nibelung. When their father, the brave Gibich, had died, their mother, Grimhilde, had wedded the Nibelung, and after a while had died herself, leaving wild, dark Hagen as a brother to Gunther and Gutrune.

He was a sinister and gloomy warrior, with gleaming black eyes and blood that seemed of ice, for never did his cheek flush or his lip redden. Pale he was and cold, dark-haired and sad, and his heart was black and cruel. He, too, was working to obtain the Rhinegold.

One day Gunther, sitting on a high throne beside his sister, asked Hagen what greater wealth could belong to the Gibichungs; what deed their chief could do that would aid the good fortune of the race and its vassals.

Hagen answered that it would be fitting for the head of the Gibichungs to wed, and he craftily told Gunther of the fire-encirled rock where dwelt the fair maiden, Brünnhilde. The fire could only be conquered, he said, by Siegfried, the Volsung, who would make a fitting husband for Gutrune.

Now, Hagen knew that Siegfried had already won the Walküre; but he was laying a plot, and the plot was wicked and deep. He told Gunther that Siegfried would go through the fire and bring Brünnhilde to the Rhine Chief if he could be given a magic-potion — a potion that would make him love Gutrune.

While they spoke of these things, a horn was heard, in the distance at first, but coming nearer and nearer. Soon a boat came down the river Rhine—a wide barge—holding a horse and a tall man in bright armor. Siegfried, in his travels through the world, had heard of the Gibichungs, and had come to see the great Rhine Chief, Gunther. As the boat touched the shore, he sprang from it, and hailed the warrior, in loud tones, asking if he would be friend or enemy. In answer, Gunther said that his house, his lands, his people were all at the service of the hero whose fame had reached even the hall of the Gibichungs; and Siegfried offered the strength of his arm and the might of his sword for Gunther's defence and aid at all times.

So they made a vow, promising to remain true to each other, as heroes and brave men should.

" I have heard that you hold the Nibelungs' hoard," said Hagen, when Gutrune, at a sign from him, had left the hall, and the three warriors were alone.

" I left it in the cavern," said Siegfried. " I

cared nothing for the Gold.   This is all I took "
—and he showed the Tarnhelm.   " What is its
use—do you know?"

" It is the most artful of all the Nibelung's
work," said Hagen.   " It will change you to
whatever shape you will, and carry you to the
farthest lands in a moment, if it is your wish.
Did you take any more of the hoard?"

Siegfried answered that he had carried away
a Ring, but that it was now worn by a beautiful woman.

Even as he spoke, Gutrune, the fair lady of the
Gibichungs, came out from her room at one side
of the hall, bearing a drinking-horn, which she
offered to Siegfried.   It was customary in those
days that a maiden should offer wine to a guest
coming to the house of her race.   So Siegfried,
without a thought, lifted the horn and drank the
mixture, saying softly to himself: " Brünnhilde,
I drink to you !"

But, alas! it was not wine that was in the
drinking-horn, but the love-potion—the terrible
magic potion—which, as it touched the hero's
lips, laid a cloud upon his memory and a fire
within his heart, so that he straightway forgot
Brünnhilde and loved only Gutrune, the lady of
the Gibichungs.

GUTRUNE AND SIEGFRIED

As he gazed passionately upon her, she turned away, filled, perhaps, with momentary regret for what she had done, and left the hall in silence.

When she had gone, Siegfried stood looking after her for a moment, and then, arousing himself from his reverie, turned to Gunther, asking if he were married.

The Rhine Chief replied that he had never wed, because only one bride would satisfy him, and she was out of reach of even his valor; for she was surrounded by fire, and only he who could pass through the blaze could win her.

Merrily, Siegfried replied that he would go through the flame and bring the bride to Gunther if he might have in payment Gutrune for his wife.

And the two heroes went through a ceremony, very binding in those days, which was called the Oath of Brotherhood. It meant that they must remain as faithful to each other as though they were really brothers, and that should one prove false to his vow the other would have the right to kill him.

Then the two entered the boat and went away down the Rhine, Siegfried to take Gunther's shape, with the aid of the Tarnhelm, and go through the fire to win the maiden; Gunther

to wait on the banks of the Rhine until Siegfried brought him the bride, and then took his
own shape once more.

Hagen, left alone in the hall, mused deeply as
night drew near.

"Siegfried, unknowing, brings his own bride
to the Rhine. *He brings me the Ring!*" He
paused, and then continued, in tones of bitter
scorn: "Little as I deem you all, you brave
partners and happy companions—small as you
are, and as I hold your natures—you still may
serve the need of the Nibelung's son!"

Motif of the Love-Potion

Motif of the Magic-fire Circle

## CHAPTER II

### THE WALKÜRES' ROCK ONCE MORE

As afternoon darkened into evening Brünnhilde sat on her high rock looking at the Ring
on her finger with loving eyes, and thinking tenderly of the hero who had placed it there, and
who was perhaps, even then, leaving the paths
of men to come to her side once more.

Suddenly a flash of lightning appeared across
the sky and a clap of thunder sounded far away.
Strange sounds broke the stillness, sounds well
remembered by her: the hoofs of wind-horses
speeding through the clouds, the whistling of
rushing blasts, the ring of steel armor. Starting
up in wild excitement, she saw a black thunder-
cloud rushing towards the rock.

8

"Brünnhilde! Sister! Are you asleep or awake?" called the clear voice of one of the warrior goddesses, as a war-horse sprang to earth from the midst of the clouds.

With a cry of joy Brünnhilde ran to meet the Walküre, saying:

"Waltraute, truest sister, welcome!" and asking tenderly about the rest of the maidens and her father Wotan.

But Waltraute was sad and anxious, and seemed in fearful haste. She interrupted Brünnhilde's passionate description of her hero and her happiness in his love by sad words of the gloom that reigned in Walhalla. She told the story of the hewing of the World-Ash, the fagots piled high about the great palace; of the gods and heroes assembled in awe. She spoke of Wotan sitting in silence holding his broken spear in his hand.

She said that once, and once only, had he spoken, and that he had then said: "When the Rhine daughters gain from Brünnhilde the Ring the world will be released from the power of the spell."

Waltraute begged Brünnhilde to give her the Ring, so that she, Waltraute, might carry it to the Rhine Maidens.

"If you wish, you may ward off the shadow

of the gods," said the Walküre, kneeling at her
sister's feet. But Brünnhilde looked at her as
though in a trance.

"Like a sorrowful dream it seems — this that
you tell me. I do not understand it. I am no
longer one of the gods. You, pale sister—what
have you to do with me?"

Passionately, Waltraute asked for the Ring
which she wore, but Brünnhilde replied that it
was Siegfried's love-gift, and that she would
never give it up. Again Waltraute besought
her, for the sake of the gods, the bright mighty
gods, who were going to destruction, to give up
the magic circlet.

Brünnhilde answered quietly that she prized
love more than the welfare of all the gods, and
that the Ring was dearer to her than the palace
of Walhalla ; and she bade Waltraute be gone,
refusing once for all to give up Siegfried's
gift.

"Woe! woe!" wailed the Walküre, speeding
wildly away. "Woe for you, sister! Woe for
the gods in Walhalla! Woe!"

She was gone, amid thunder and rushing
winds.

Sitting again on the rock alone, Brünnhilde
looked down to where the guarding fire-circle

burned brighter and brighter. A horn-call sounded in the distance.

"Siegfried!" cried Brünnhilde, rushing forward.

But who was that who sprang from out the fire and stood before her? Not Siegfried, surely, but some stranger — a stranger with face partly masked by a curious helmet of some sort.

No wonder that she did not recognize her hero in the man before her, who, by the aid of the Tarnhelm, bore the semblance of Gunther, the Gibichung. He told her that he had come to take her away with him and marry her; and when she ordered him to yield before the strength of the mighty Ring on her finger, he caught her hand and tore the circlet from it, placing it on his own.

"Now yield to me! You must be my wife," he commanded; and, weak and powerless, Brünnhilde was conquered and led away by the warrior, who was none other than Siegfried — had she but known it!—Siegfried, her hero, who did not remember her at all, and only looked upon her as the bride of his brother-hero Gunther, the bride that must be delivered safely into the real Gibichung's hand.

LES FILLES DE BIENFILÂTRE

For Siegfried cared nothing for her himself, and thought only of the fair maiden down in the great hall built upon the shore of the Rhine— Gutrune, the lady of the Gibichungs.

And that was how the Nibelung's spell again brought sorrow and misery to the wearer of the Rhinegold's Ring.

Tarnhelm Motif

Gutrune Motif

Motif of Revenge

## CHAPTER III

### THE RHINE CHIEF'S BRIDE

IT was night on the Rhine. Hagen sat asleep before the hall of the Gibichungs, leaning against a pillar. Before him crouched his Nibelung father, Alberich, who had come to speak with him through his dreams.

They spoke of the Rhinegold in mysterious undertones, Hagen in the voice of one who talks in sleep. They spoke of the Dusk of the Gods which drew near so quickly, and of the might which would be theirs when the Ring fell into their hands. And until dawn came they concocted plots deep and cruel.

Then the Nibelung's small, dark figure disappeared in a pale mist, and all that was left of him was the echo of his voice, as he called, faintly, while vanishing:

" Be true, Hagen, my son; be true! Be true! True!" The voice died away into silence.

As the dawn broke and the rising sun was mirrored brightly in the Rhine, Hagen awoke with a start. At the same moment Siegfried appeared, saying that he had hastened to the hall of the Gibichungs with the aid of the Tarn-helm, leaving Gunther and his bride to follow in a barge up the Rhine.

As Gutrune came out to meet him, he hailed her exultantly, saying that he had won her as wife when he brought the wild mountain - maid to her brother. He told her and Hagen the tale of how he had gone through the fire and found the woman within the enchanted circle, and had conquered her, and had brought her to Gunther, who had waited at the foot of the mountain. The only thing that he did not tell them was that he had torn the Ring from the woman's fin-ger, and so vanquished her. Strange to say, he had forgotten that as completely as he had for-gotten his old love for Brünnhilde and his first journey through the fire. Now, when he looked at the bright circlet on his finger, he remembered that it was one which he had obtained at Hate Hole, but had forgotten that it had ever left his hand.  So that was the beginning of more sorrow.

Siegfried and Gutrune went into the hall together, and Hagen called the vassals about him from far and wide to welcome the bride to her new home on the Rhine.  When the barge came slowly up the river, strong warriors plunged into the water to meet it, and dragged the boat close to the shore.  From the hall came Gutrune, full of welcome and kindness.  For you know she had no idea it was Brünnhilde whom she had caused the hero to forget, and she was really glad to greet her brother's bride.  At her side walked Siegfried, and they were followed by innumerable women who had come trooping out to behold the new lady of the Gibichungs.

But, as Gunther led his pale, sad bride from the boat, she suddenly stood still, trembling and shuddering, and staring with wild, bewildered eyes at Siegfried.  Her voice shook and her face was as white as death as she asked how he came there with Gutrune; and when he showed that he had totally forgotten her and looked upon her only as Gunther's bride, she staggered and sank into the young hero's arms, whispering, faintly and sorrowfully:

" Siegfried knows me not !"

Calling to Gunther to come near, the Volsung pointed to him and bade poor Brünnhilde arouse herself, for the great chief's sake. But, as Siegfried stretched out his hand, she saw the Ring, and, starting wildly up, asked furiously how he came by it — saying that Gunther had torn it from her on the Walküres' rock, and demanding of Gunther why he had given it to Siegfried.

Now, of course, the Rhine Chief had never even seen the Ring, and thought, not unnaturally, that Siegfried had taken it from Brünnhilde and then kept it for himself from a feeling of greed and a desire to possess it. The young hero, when questioned, merely answered that it was one he had found at Hate Hole, and that he had won it from no woman, but a monster worm which he had killed. And he thought that he was telling the whole truth, for it was all that he could remember.

But Brünnhilde, who knew nothing of the magic-potion, saw in his words the deepest and most terrible deceit, and she burst into such rage and despair that Siegfried declared that he would try to satisfy her by swearing the Spear-Oath.

So Hagen held out his spear, and Siegfried placed his hand upon the point and declared by the haft of war that he had never harmed the woman, or been for a moment false to Gunther, and bade that very spear bring him death if he had.

Breaking into the circle which the warriors made around Siegfried, Brünnhilde declared him a traitor and deceiver, and called down the vengeance of the gods upon his head.

For her heart was broken, poor Brünnhilde! and she hardly knew what she said or did; so that when Siegfried and the others ceased trying to pacify her and left her alone with Gunther and Hagen, and when the latter crept up to her and said that he would avenge her wrongs and kill the hero who had made her love him and had then deserted her, she told him how to do it. She said that she had placed divine spells of protection upon every part of his body except his back.

"For I knew," said Brünnhilde, with momentary tenderness, "that he was too brave to ever, in flight, turn that to an enemy."

"At his back shall my spear-point strike!" said Hagen, exultantly. "In his back shall he be wounded unto death!"

Raising her arms towards the sky, Brunnhilde broke into wild, passionate words of revenge.

GUNTHER AND BRÜNNHILDE

For she had almost lost her reason through the shock of sorrow at finding Siegfried false to her, and she declared that that was the sacrifice that was needed to lift the sorrow off so many hearts; that was the one great deed that must bring relief after so much misery. Earth and heaven cried aloud for one thing, she said — Siegfried's death.

As she stood, almost transfigured by her own words, sounds of joy and merriment drew near, and the wedding procession of Siegfried and Gutrune passed by. Gunther caught Brünnhilde's hand and drew her into the crowd of men and women, and she passed on with the other bridal couple to be married.

Loudly and merrily rang the laughter, and the sounds of festivity rose high. But Hagen, like a dark, evil spirit, laughed, because he seemed at last so near to his desires.

Motif of the Rhine-Maidens' Prophecy

Fate Motif

## CHAPTER IV

### ON THE BANKS OF THE RHINE

WHERE the steep rocks led down to the river
Rhine, and the low shrubs grew in green luxu-
riance, where the wildest part of the wild forest
was mirrored in the water, came the three water-
fairies, Woglinde, Flosshilde, and Wellgunde, to
sing in the quiet, golden light of the late afternoon.  They sang sorrowfully and regretfully of
their lost treasure ; they circled like wind-ripples
upon the surface of the Rhine, and tossed the

bright drops of water about with a soft, splash-
ing sound as of tiny bells. The river murmured
like a harp lightly played upon by fairy fingers, and the voices of the nymphs were as
sweet as the tones of the wind moving through
the rushes.

To this lovely, magic-haunted spot came Siegfried, looking for a bear which he had wounded during a hunt, and had tracked through the
woods. The nymphs began to talk to him, and
as he answered merrily they drew nearer to the
rock where he stood, telling him that they would
see that he found his bear if he would, in payment, give them the Ring that he wore upon his
finger.

Laughingly, he answered that he had slain a
dragon before he could obtain that Ring, and
that it would be foolish to give it up now for
the sake of a bear.

After a few more merry words the nymphs became suddenly serious. Rising together to the
surface of the water, they raised their arms towards him and spoke solemn words of prophecy. They told him that sadness awaited him ;
that the Ring would bring him nothing but
ill-hap ; that it was made of the stolen Rhinegold, and that a spell had been laid upon it

that brought sorrow and death to whoever pos·
sessed it.

"As the monster worm fell," said the Rhine
Maidens, slowly, "so will you fall—and soon!
Give it to us, that we may hide it in the river!
For that alone can break the spell."

And, as Siegfried laughingly shook his head,
they continued to plead still more earnestly.
They bade him avoid the spell, saying that its
history had been woven into the Norns' great
rope; that it must be shunned and feared. But
Siegfried scoffed at the Norns and the rope, and
said that Fafner had warned him of this danger
long ago; that he had no fear of his life, and
would freely fling that away.

"Farewell, Siegfried!" said the Rhine Maidens, as they turned to leave him. "A stately
woman will soon possess your circlet. She will
better do our bidding. Let us go to her!"

They swam swiftly away, leaving Siegfried
laughing on the shore. For he thought noth·
ing of their words, believing their prophecies
to have been threats because he would not give
them what they wished.

Laughing still, he blew a long call on his horn,
which was answered on all sides by the other
hunters, who soon made their appearance, most

of them carrying game of some sort — bear or
deer; and Hagen, who was one of the first to
come into the little glen down by the Rhine,
made sport of Siegfried, because he, the best
hunter of them all, had no booty to show for his
day's sport.

Siegfried laughingly told them about the three
Rhine Maidens who had warned him of his ap-
proaching death; and Gunther, moving apart
from the others with a curious shadow and sadness on his face, started terribly, while Hagen
merely laughed a harsh, revengeful laugh.

Gunther did not forget his Oath of Brotherhood; and, though he believed that Siegfried
had deceived him, he hated to harm him, or allow
him to be harmed, without better cause. He
shuddered and shook his head when the young
hero brought him the horn of wine. The rest
of the hunters flung themselves down under the
trees, and drank merrily and rested in the deepening golden light of the afternoon, but Gunther
sat apart from them, gloomy and silent, like one
who dreamed sad dreams, and could not arouse
himself.

At last, Siegfried, noticing his depression, said
that he would tell him the story of his boyhood,
if it would amuse and cheer him.

And sitting down on the stump of a great tree, with his shield and weapons at his feet, and on all sides the warriors listening eagerly to his words, the young Volsung began his tale, and Hagen stood near, leaning on his spear, a look of grim expectation on his dark face.

It was of Mime that Siegfried spoke first, Mime and the life in the cave; the forging of Nothung, and finally the journey to Hate Hole, and the slaying of the monster worm, Fafner.

He told how the Dragon's blood had given him power to understand the language of birds; and, as he spoke, memories of the soft woodland voices and the rustling of the trees passed tenderly across his mind. He told of the winning of the Rhinegold Ring and the Tarnhelm, of the treachery of Mime, and of how he had killed him with Nothung.

Then he paused, for Hagen came up to him with a drinking-horn filled with wine, which he bade him swallow, saying it would help to clear his memory. Siegfried raised it to his lips and drank, and Hagen stood near, leaning on his spear, and smiling grimly. For the wine had in it something that would, indeed, bring back the young hero's memory, and Hagen knew that, when he remembered Brünnhilde, he would

HAGEN AND SIEGFRIED

be as one deaf and blind to all else, and would so prove an easy victim.

Siegfried put down the drinking-horn, and, after a moment's silence, resumed his tale, while the memory of the forest sounds passed softly and constantly across his brain. He told, in tender tones, how the bird had sung to him of a glorious bride sleeping amid fire far away; and of how he had passed through the enchanted flame-circle, and, with a kiss, awakened her from her long sleep; and he spoke her name with such love and tenderness that even Hagen's wicked heart should have been touched for a moment; but he only stood leaning on his spear and smiling—always smiling—as one smiles who has knowledge greater than his fellows.

Gunther started up wildly as Siegfried whispered the name of "Brünnhilde"; for the Rhine Chief understood all now, and realized in that short time what deep wickedness it must have been that had parted the noble Volsung and his bride. There had been no deceit, no treachery, no broken Oath of Brotherhood — none of the wickedness had been on the young hero's side. Gunther dropped his head in horror.

But Hagen took a step forward.

"See you those Ravens?" he said, slowly, point-

9

ing to two great black birds flying upward from the Rhine. They were Wotan's King-Ravens, which had been sent out to bring tidings back to Walhalla, and which were returning there with news that the Dusk of the Gods was at hand. Siegfried turned to gaze after them as they flew. It was growing late. The yellow afternoon light was deepening to red gold. The sun was setting. The Ravens flew away, their broad black wings bathed in the ruddy light, and it was like the light of a great fire.

"They arouse in me revenge!" cried Hagen, and he raised his spear and stabbed the young Volsung in the back. Siegfried staggered wildly; and then, raising his shield, tried to crush Hagen with it. But then even his great strength left him, and he fell back upon the ground, while the warriors drew near with exclamations of horror and faces on which a great awe had fallen.

"I have been revenged," said Hagen, and passed up the rocks and out of sight amid the growing dusk. The sunset was as red as blood now. There was an ominous look in its lurid light— yet a strange peace also. It lay on the head and figure of the young hero like a king's crown and robe.

In the hush that had fallen, Siegfried raised himself upon his arm and spoke.

He spoke of Brünnhilde, his bride; again he seemed to be on the Walküres' rock; again she lay before him asleep; again he awakened her with a kiss. He seemed to look into her eyes, to hear her voice; she was his once more.

And with the words "Brünnhilde beckons to me! Greeting!" Siegfried sank back and died. And the last light from the setting sun went out of the sky.

It was very dark—very dark and silent. The warriors raised the hero upon their shoulders and bore him up the rocks. After a while the moon rose, and the pale light touched the helmets of the men and Siegfried's armor as the procession passed up through the shadows. A mist was rising from the Rhine, and it was very still.

Siegfried was dead, the last of his race — the noble race of Volsungs. He was the bravest of them all, this son of Siegmund and Sieglinde, who had so loved each other. He had done many great deeds with his good sword Nothung. He had been a courageous man and the highest hero in the world, and he had won the love of Brünnhilde, the noblest woman ever born. And he was dead—Siegfried, the Volsung.

Death Motif

Motif of the Dusk of the Gods

## CHAPTER V

### THE LAST TWILIGHT

ALONE through the great hall of the Gibichungs wandered Gutrune, awaiting Siegfried's
return from the hunt. Going to Brünnhilde's
chamber in the hope of finding a companion
in her anxiety, she saw that the room was emp-
ty, and remembered that she had seen, some
time before, a woman's figure descend towards
the Rhine. As she thought of her brother's
wild, strange bride, Gutrune shuddered. She
moved restlessly about the hall, listening for
the clear horn-call that always heralded the
coming of the Volsung.

Suddenly, Hagen appeared with a look of triumph on his dark, evil face; and, directly after-

wards, many people came running, in wild confusion, carrying torches, and lamenting the hero's
death. And, finally, came the warriors bearing
Siegfried upon a great bier.

With wails of anguish, Gutrune flung herself
on her knees beside her hero, and pushed Gunther away wildly when he strove to comfort
her, calling him the murderer of her husband.

But Gunther denied the charge, and pointed
to Hagen, accusing him, in heart-broken tones, of
having slain their hero. Hagen answered, with
calm defiance, that he had, indeed, killed Siegfried, and that he now demanded as booty the
Ring that gleamed upon the finger of the Volsung.

Fiercely, Gunther claimed the circlet for his
sister, as widow's dower. Hagen sprang forward
to attack him, and the half-brothers fought wildly together for the Rhinegold Ring. At last,
with an exultant gesture, Hagen raised his sword
above his head; for, at his feet lay Gunther, the
Gibichung—dead.

"The Ring!" cried the Nibelung's son, and
he sprang to the bier. But, ere he could touch
Siegfried's hand where gleamed the circlet, it
raised itself threateningly. And even Hagen
started back in terror. On all sides people trem-

bled with fear and horror. Gutrune screamed wildly as her eyes encountered her brother's body on the ground.

Into this place of sorrow and confusion came a tall woman, robed in white, with a face most beautiful in its gentleness and strength ; and before so calm and tender a gaze the crowd parted, as though in awe, to let the woman pass.

It was Brünnhilde, who had heard from the water-maidens everything that had happened on the shores of the Rhine. She understood all now. She understood that he had never been false, knowingly ; that his last loving words had been of her—and her alone. And she had come, with her great wisdom and her great love, to bring peace to the turbulent hearts gathered about Siegfried's bier.

She stood for a long time gazing down on the face of her hero—"The highest hero of worlds," she called him. She looked around her and smiled upon the confusion and sorrow, and, before the tenderness and solemn sweetness of that smile, the confusion seemed to die away and the sorrow seemed but as something too small to be shown.

Piteously, Gutrune sobbed out words of regret for the wrong which had been done Brünnhilde, and reproached Hagen for his share in the plot. But Brünnhilde hardly heard.

In slow, solemn tones, she ordered a funeral pyre to be lighted on the banks of the Rhine, and, bending over Siegfried, she spoke tenderly of his love and of his nobility and truth.

Then, turning away, she raised her arms on high and broke into sublime words, in which she reproached Wotan for his wrath, and added that already his Ravens were on their way to Walhalla to carry the long-deferred tidings of the last Twilight—so close at hand.

"Rest! Rest! O gods!" she said, softly, and paused. She turned towards Siegfried again and drew the Ring from his finger. Then she spoke to the three invisible Rhine children, and told them to take the circlet from her ashes when she had been burned with her hero.

The pyre was erected now, and Siegfried's body had been placed upon it. Grani was led in, and Brünnhilde laid her arm upon his neck tenderly, and spoke of the warrior who was dead and of the leap into the flames they were both about to take. Wildly, she seized a torch and lighted the pyre; and, as the flames rose high, she sprang upon the horse's back and raised him for a leap.

" Siegfried ! Siegfried ! See !" she cried—and her voice echoed both far and near. " Gladly greets thee thy bride !"

Into the flames sprang Grani, the stanch war-horse, and the Walküre was gone from the eyes of men forever. But, behold ! Her deed brought release from the sin and sorrow of many years.

The flames, rising high and higher, made a great fiery wall between the earth and sky. The Rhine Maidens swam up to the shore and caught a bright circlet lying near in the midst of a heap of ashes. Hagen, springing after it, was lost in the Rhine's rushing waters forever.

But now a wonderful sight met the gaze of the awe-stricken people crouching in the hall of the Gibichungs.

In the high heavens, Walhalla's stately towers appeared in a bright ring of fire. The fagots made from the World-Ash had at last caught fire. Dimly could be seen the great array of gods and heroes awaiting the Last Twilight, and the end.

Wildly, and still more wildly, leaped the flames. Walhalla was surrounded with red fire—it could no longer be seen. A fearful light glowed upon earth and heaven.

Lo! the Dusk of the Gods was come.

\*      \*      \*      \*      \*

And that was how the Last Twilight came to Walhalla, and how Brünnhilde lifted the spell off the world and expiated the old sins of so many years before.

And that was how the Golden Age came to an end, and a better and nobler era of truth and happiness reigned upon the earth.

So the enchanted Rhinegold came back to the hands of its first guardians—the maidens of the river; and, after great sorrow and turmoil, there was at last peace.

Motif of Brünnhilde's Expiation

**FINIS**